C000218017

The Demon of the Dusk

The rediscovered cases of Sherlock Holmes Book 1

Arthur Hall

Copyright © Arthur Hall 1997, 2017

The right of Arthur Hall to be identified as the author of this work has been asserted by him in accordance with the Copyright, Designs and Patents Act 1998.

All rights reserved. No reproduction, copy or transmission of this publication may be made without express prior written permission. No paragraph of this publication may be reproduced, copied or transmitted except with express prior written permission or in accordance with the provisions of the Copyright Act 1956 (as amended). Any person who commits any unauthorised act in relation to this publication may be liable to criminal prosecution and civil claims for damage.

All characters appearing in this work are fictitious or used fictitiously. Except for certain historical personages, any resemblance to real persons, living or dead, is purely coincidental. The opinions expressed herein are those of the author and not of MX Publishing.

Arthur Hall was born in Aston, Birmingham, UK, in 1944. He discovered his interest in writing during his schooldays, along with a love of fictional adventure and suspense.

His first novel "Sole Contact" was an espionage story about an ultra-secret government department known as "Sector Three" and was followed, to date, by three sequels.

Other works include four "rediscovered" cases from the files of Sherlock Holmes, two collections of bizarre short stories and two modern adventure novels, as well as several contributions to the continuing anthology, "The MX Book of New Sherlock Holmes Stories".

His only ambition, apart from being published more widely, is to attend the premier of a film based on one of his novels, possibly at The Odeon, Leicester Square.

He lives in the West Midlands, United Kingdom, where he often walks other people's dogs as he attempts to create new plots.

The author welcomes comments and observations about his work, at arthurhall7777@aol.co.uk

By the same author:

Sole Contact

A Faint and Distant Threat

The Sagittarius Ring

Controlled Descent

The Final Strategy

Facets of Fantasy

Curious Tales

The Plain Face of Truth

The One Hundred per Cent Society - A second rediscovered case from the files of Sherlock Holmes.

The Secret Assassin – A third rediscovered case from the files of Sherlock Holmes.

The Phantom Killer – A fourth rediscovered case from the files of Sherlock Holmes.

CONTENTS

1 The Jester of Armington Keep

2 Theobald Grange

3 Into Thin Air

4 Concerning Flying Men

5 Of Cyclists and Unwelcome Visitors

6 Two Dead Men

7 Her Ladyship's Distress

8 The Stranger in the Wood

9 Dr Phineas Turville

10 Death of an Unknown Woman

11 The Phantom of Maybell Wood

12 Some Reconstructions

Chapter One - The Jester of Armington Keep

My friend Mr Sherlock Holmes was never, by any description, a follower of convention or of fashion. He was clothed, always, in garments appropriate for a given occasion or time of day, but when gentlemen's collars began to be worn with a longer point, or their trousers cut a little more generously, Holmes would ignore the changes, fleeting as they usually were, and continue his existence as before.

So it was with places. Sometimes he would read, in one of the numerous newspapers he received regularly, that this restaurant or that gentleman's club was a popular place to be seen, more often than not because someone of fame or notoriety was known to frequent the establishment. He found this distasteful, likening the practice to the herd instinct commonly displayed by animals.

Usually, Holmes shunned society. Indeed, he rarely entered any club in London, never doing so at all unless as part of a current enquiry or investigation.

My surprise was therefore complete as we emerged from a violin recital at St James Hall, Piccadilly, on a fine early April evening when my suggestion that we delay our return to Baker Street long enough to visit Brenner's, the well-known and fashionable tea rooms, was approved.

"It is just off the Strand I think, Watson."

"But not far, I have been given directions."

He gave me an amused, sidelong glance. "I hope Mrs Watson was specific, so that we do not find ourselves wandering the district until we chance to come upon the place."

"Holmes, I did not say that Brenner's was recommended to me by my wife."

"Indeed, you did not, but I recall that a faint aroma of an unfamiliar blend of fresh coffee clung to your morning coat on each of the recent occasions when we have met. By your own admission during our conversations, your social life has been somewhat restricted of late. You have for some little time visited regularly only my rooms in Baker Street, apart from your surgery, where I know you always drink tea. Therefore, my dear fellow, you drank the coffee at home. I have no doubt that Mrs Watson purchased it while at Brenner's on an afternoon outing with her friends from the Women's Circle."

This, I thought, was too much, even from him. "Ingenious, but you overlook the obvious."

His eyes shone with an amused twinkle as he raised his eyebrows. "How so?"

"Because," I retorted triumphantly, "I could have called in to a coffee house anywhere, returning more than once if it were to my liking, at any time in the course of my travels about London. Would that not explain all that you have said?"

Holmes smiled. "No, Watson, that will not do. That particular fragrance was unknown to me, but it has the harshness of the newly popular South American mixtures. According to yesterday's newspapers, Brenner's is at present sole importers of these in London, and you have already indicated that you have never been there."

"So you concluded that both the mixture and the tea rooms were introduced to me by my wife." I applauded him. "Bravo, Holmes, as always you are correct."

We made use of a passing cab for the short distance, and left it a few paces from the entrance. With several other men and two or three couples, we walked through the arched doorway.

We deposited our hats and coats and left the foyer, to find ourselves in a cavernous room that was almost completely walled with mirrors. Rows of tables, most of them occupied, stretched before us past white marble pillars. Waiters hurried between them, laden with steaming food and drink.

"I must say that I approve of Mrs Watson's taste as to our surroundings," Holmes remarked. "The décor is exquisite, and the spaciousness enhanced by the clever use of mirrors."

We were soon seated near the edge of the room, next to one of the wide pillars, and I picked up a menu card from the starched white tablecloth. Already I could see why my wife had been so favourably impressed, for the bill of fare, like the room itself, compared well with many of the capital's finest restaurants.

"What will you eat, Holmes?"

He studied the card. "Today my appetite is not very great. Some of these hot scones perhaps, with butter and some preserve. And," he glanced at me, "a cup of the South American coffee, of course."

"I will have the same," I said to the waiter who had arrived and written down Holmes' order as it was dictated.

"I may write a monograph on the peculiarities of different varieties of coffee," he mused when the man had left us, "as I did on tobacco, should such a paper ever promise to be useful."

Not for the first time recently, I studied his appearance carefully. Resplendent in his evening clothes, Holmes looked much healthier than of late. His nerves were apparently stronger, his complexion more ruddy, though this was always pale by normal standards, and his eyes sharply alive. Earlier I observed that he had adopted once more the upright posture of old, which made him appear taller than ever, and the gaunt expression brought on by overwork was gradually fading from his features. I could, to my immense relief, see no sign of a return to the cocaine bottle, which he had at last forsaken at my insistence. Finally, I decided that he was now quite recovered from the taxing exertions undergone during the affairs of the Peruvian Quintet and the Demise of Mr Antoine Valderer, as well as the unexpected recurrence of a situation from his days in Montague Street, about which I have been sworn to secrecy.

The food arrived, and we said little as we ate. His restless eyes took in our surroundings, his gaze swept over the leaning palms, the aspidistras and climbing shrubs and the gleaming brass of the gas chandeliers.

"Well, Holmes," I said at length, "was the South American mixture to your taste?"

"It is a little coarse," he said absently, "but I shall suggest to Mrs Hudson that that we might find it enjoyable at breakfast."

His detached air caused me to glance at him as I pushed away my plate. He stared fixedly at the image in the mirrored wall behind me. I looked past him to see two couples leaving their table together, noticing that one of the women, a striking, black-haired girl attired in a scarlet gown, had halted abruptly and was staring in our direction. She approached her escort who had moved aside to allow her to pass, and spoke to him in a whisper, so that he was obliged to incline his head in order to hear. His reaction to her words was one of surprise and disappointment, but then he bowed once before leaving her to re-join their companions. After a moment the three looked uncertainly back, but the girl made no acknowledgement and they left her standing alone.

"A friend of yours, I imagine, Watson?" Holmes gave me a quick look from beneath raised eyebrows. "I hope so, since she seems set on renewing your acquaintance."

"I have never before set eyes on the young lady," I told him with some embarrassment.

But it did seem as if she had left her companions for reasons somehow connected with us, for as soon as it was certain that they had departed she turned and walked directly to our table.

"Mr Sherlock Holmes?" she enquired, addressing us both.

My embarrassment vanished and my glance at Holmes held a hint of irony, but his attention was captured already.

4

"I am he," was his reply, "and this is Dr Watson. How may we assist you?"

"Gentlemen," she said with apparent nervousness, "I have great need of your help. Or of yours at least, Mr Holmes, if it is at all possible."

I saw his face light up at once. "You may speak as freely in Dr Watson's presence as in mine, since he has been instrumental to many of my past successes. But please, be seated and we will discuss your problem, unless you would prefer to call on us at Baker Street, tomorrow morning?"

She shook her head. "Now would be better, if you will permit it. My business is of an urgent and curious nature."

"Very well, then." With that he rose and held a chair for her, re-seating himself when she was settled. "May we order something for you?"

"Thank you, no." She smiled quickly. "I have already eaten with my friends, whom you observed in the mirror."

Holmes beamed at her. "You also are observant, I fancy. But tell me, why did you not accost us in Hyde Park yesterday? Since you had followed us for some little distance, I fully expected you to do so, but you disappeared by the time we reached the Serpentine. As we continued our walk, a coach with drawn blinds passed us. I presume you were its passenger?"

I turned to him in astonishment, for I had noticed nothing unusual during that short excursion. With a movement of his hand, he indicated that I should keep silent.

The young lady averted her eyes and her cheeks reddened. "I had thought myself unobserved. My intention was to call upon you in your rooms, but my nerves got the better of me. I followed you, trying to find the courage to approach, as I saw you leave Baker Street."

"I was aware of it from the first."

5

"Forgive me," she raised her eyes to look into Holmes' face, "but the matter on which I wish to consult you would seem ridiculous to some, laughable, even. To others it would appear fantastical, to be dismissed as foolishness, yet it is of great importance to me that it be resolved. My aunt's sanity is at stake."

"I understand your position," Holmes said gently. "You were torn between inviting scorn upon yourself and a pressing need to take some action to relieve your aunt's anxieties. Allow me to reassure you, for Dr Watson and myself are far from unaccustomed to investigating events that appear at first to be without explanation, the seemingly impossible. Indeed, it is these singular features, which are not always apparent at first, that usually prove most interesting. Try to put your embarrassment aside and collect the facts as you know them, clearly in your mind. Then, when you are ready, pray tell us what you can."

A few moments passed, during which the young lady composed herself, her expression relieved at the understanding that Holmes had shown.

"I am Miss Florence Monkton," she began presently. "Your reputation is known to me through a friend of my late father, whom you once had occasion to help."

"May I know the name of this friend?" Holmes enquired.

"It was Mr Cavendish Stroud, of Wyatt, Greenway & Decker, in Streatham."

"Ah, the Feldenberg blackmail scandal. That was some years ago, I trust it has no connection with your present difficulty?"

"None." The light from the gas lamps shone on her raven-black hair as she shook her head. "The events that have caused so much distress concern my aunt, Lady Heminworth, of Theobald Grange, in Warwickshire. As well as forcing her to the edge of madness, they have resulted in the death of my uncle and one of my cousins."

Holmes' eyes were fixed upon her. I could tell from his altered attitude, now with his head thrust forward, that she had captured his entire attention. "Please continue. Your narrative promises much of interest."

"This tale," she said after some recollection, "begins about two years ago. At that time, I lived with my mother, as I do now, in Cornwall, not far from Truro. You will therefore understand, gentlemen, that all I tell you has been pieced together from conversations with my aunt and others in her household, which have taken place during several visits to Theobald Grange since that time."

"Your mother and Lady Heminworth are sisters, then?" Holmes asked.

"They are, although they have seen little of each other for some years now. My father, you see, had to be nursed throughout a long illness."

"Quite so."

"In those days, my aunt lived with her husband, Sir Joseph Heminworth, and their eldest son, Robert. Their younger son, Donald, who had been in the South African diamond fields for years, suddenly reappeared, much to the surprise and happiness of the family. The joy did not last, however, for more than a day or two. Then, for reasons as yet undisclosed to me, Sir Joseph sank into a sullen and morose state, seeing no one and taking his meals in his study. My aunt was greatly troubled by this most uncharacteristic behaviour, and resorted to astrology in an attempt to discover its cause." She paused, probably to judge our reaction to the mention of her aunt's extraordinary action, before proceeding cautiously. "I should explain that this sort of thing is something of an obsession with her, no doubt because of her exceedingly nervous and superstitious nature. Sir Joseph usually considered the practice a harmless eccentricity, something of a joke."

This revelation had no effect on Holmes' keen interest. "Most interesting," he murmured, "but not at all unique."

"My aunt has had this fascination for things mystical since childhood, an interest shared with no one else in the house. As it happened, her astrological studies revealed nothing as far as Sir Joseph was concerned. When he emerged from his isolation, it was evident from his haggard countenance that he had suffered grievously and had come to some sort of decision at great personal cost. That night, when dinner was over, he announced with much emotion that Donald was to leave Theobald Grange forever, departing early the next morning.

"Of course, my aunt and Robert were shocked at this and pressed Sir Joseph for an explanation, but all he would reveal was that Donald had committed an act which, should he be allowed to remain with us, would bring lasting disgrace upon the Heminworth family. It transpired that he had chosen to spend the remainder of his life in Australia, among the settlers and convicts, as a measure of atonement."

"But the details of his indiscretion were never made known?" I asked.

"Never. Sir Joseph took the secret, if one may call it that, to his grave."

Holmes looked up from his empty coffee cup. "What theory have you, yourself, formed of its nature?"

Miss Monkton shook her head helplessly. "Gambling debts, or an accident perhaps, which my cousin may have unwittingly caused before failing to behave honourably towards the unfortunate victim. All this and more has crossed my mind a thousand times. The only certainty is that the occurrence took place in South Africa, since his return from there was so recent, so I have no means of proving or disproving my suppositions."

"I perceive that Sir Joseph was a man to whom honour was of the first importance."

"Oh, yes, Mr Holmes. My uncle was a man of the breed to whom honour is everything, but a kinder and more just man I have never met. Only the welfare of his family was as close to his heart."

"Then that fact may indicate the seriousness of your cousin's failing, since only a dishonourable deed of considerable gravity would be likely to cause your uncle to take such stern measures against someone so close."

"That is where my thoughts, too, have led me," she agreed. "But all this is a mere incident in this story. There is nothing more until about six months ago, when something occurred which was the true beginning of our troubles.

"Theobald Grange, as you may have gathered, is an old house, built on the site of a castle dating from the time of the Norman Conquest. The East Tower, or what remains of it, still stands quite near to the present building, although time has rendered much of it unsafe. It is occasionally used for the storage of animal feed, which sustains the long-horned cattle in the far fields of the estate during winter, since the Tower is accessible directly from the grounds. It was there, in a cavity revealed by crumbling stonework, that a book was discovered, the scroll that began the ruin of the Heminworth family."

"This was found by Lady Heminworth herself?"

"No, by Sir Joseph's butler, Walters. I refer to the find as a book for convenience sake, but it is really the remains of several sheets of stiff parchment, fastened together and covered in ancient writing. Some of this was so faded as to be almost unreadable, but among Sir Joseph's friends were a number of eminent scholars and so a translation was eventually obtained."

"Excellent. What was learned from it?"

"The parchment contained an account of tragic incidents in the history of Armington Keep, which was the name of the original structure. This was constructed as part of the outlying fortifications of the much larger castle at Warwick, and the local village of

9

Armington Magna is called after it. The Norman knight who built the Keep, Baron Roger de Lorme, was, according to the writings, in the habit of hosting lavish feasts and banquets to entertain the local gentry and others from the neighbouring counties. As renowned as these occasions were for the abundance of food, they were still more so for the amusement they provided. It seems that, for many years, the Baron was the patron of a jester, or fool, named Brian Delacroix. This man was an accomplished musician and a teller of tales and, above all, an acrobat. Some visitors left the castle believing that they had seen him fly like a bird, so cleverly arranged were his performances. The Baron refused offers of gold, soldiers or land from those who wished to borrow or own the jester, whose fame spread across the land."

I made to ask Miss Monkton a question, but a look from Holmes kept me silent, and she continued with her train of thought unbroken.

"All was as it should have been, until the day when the jester was discovered attempting to force himself on the Baron's only daughter. Delacroix confessed his love for the maiden, who spurned him instantly, whereupon he became possessed with madness and began to beat her with harness-straps. He would surely have killed her, had not her terrified screams brought swift assistance.

"The girl was not seriously hurt, but on hearing of the occurrence the Baron flew into a furious rage, and the jester was cast into an underground cell deep beneath the castle. A headsman was sent for from London, but the man died during the journey and so the Baron, impatient as he was for Delacroix's death in order to restore his daughter's honour, took measures of his own. He caused his smiths to construct a cage of iron bands, an instrument of torture, and the jester was dragged from his cell and forced into it. He was unable to stand erect because of its constrictions and plunged into agony by the slightest movement, as the surrounding spikes pierced his flesh. The cage was borne to the battlements on the backs of soldiers and hung from the highest of the castle walls on public display. There, without food and water and exposed to the elements, he took many days to die."

"A tragic story," Holmes said.

"Horrible!" I agreed.

"Indeed, but there is more. During the days of his suffering, Delacroix is said to have called repeatedly to those passing by, many of whom mocked him. He cursed bitterly the family of Baron Roger de Lorme, and their descendants, crying out in the name of the Evil One who he claimed had bestowed his skills upon him at birth. The name of the Baron's daughter was on his lips as he expired, wishing her ten times his agonies, and then death."

"Did anything come of it?" I asked.

Miss Monkton nodded. "She died of a plague within the year."

"And so," Holmes said reasonably, "did many others within the infected area, I have no doubt. Her death cannot be taken as evidence of the fulfilment of a curse. Have there been any other happenings that could be seen as such?"

"Such ancient records as I was able to consult were vague as to dates and exact circumstances, but there is a spoken tradition, still believed locally, that has survived the centuries. It tells of several family catastrophes, any of which could have been connected with the curse, or equally have been incidents that occur in the history of most families. Of course, it is most likely to be nothing but a fanciful legend, but what is certain is that another account from a more reliable source, a museum, is a matter of historical truth. The year 1786 saw the end of the family when Quentin, the last male heir, died in a fire that all but destroyed Armington Keep, and caused the eventual rebuilding which brought about Theobald Grange. His elderly father, Roderick, died soon after, a frail and broken man who had severely depleted the estate by poor management and gambling."

11

Holmes considered this. "How then, are the present-day Heminworths connected?"

"It is thought that one of Sir Joseph's ancestors was a second cousin, but it is impossible to be certain. The line of descent is tangled, poorly recorded and incomplete, and the family has divided itself several times since the days of the Normans. Its remnants are thought to exist separately and unbeknown to each other."

"But they remain a wealthy family?"

"In a small way only, compared to former times."

"Enough for, say, a professional burglar to see them as prospective victims?"

She pondered for a moment, shaking her head slowly. "There have been times when I have suspected that their existence is barely maintained from one year to the next, but recently the situation has improved. Also, if faced with ruin, I suppose there are paintings that could be sold, or some of the land."

"Thank you. Now, I recall that you mentioned the deaths of two of your family."

"Indeed. About three months after the discovery of the book in the East Tower, Sir Joseph was found brutally strangled. The entire household was devastated of course, and completely at a loss as to the reason behind the outrage, for my uncle had no enemies."

"That cannot be quite true, evidently." Holmes rubbed his hands together, as was his habit when listening to an interesting case. "But pray tell us exactly how this unfortunate man met his end."

"He was killed in the library, quietly enjoying a cigar before retiring, as was his custom. The weapon was the cord from his dressing gown."

Holmes nodded, almost imperceptibly. "Pray continue."

"Hardly had the effects of the tragedy lifted, with Sir Joseph in his grave less than a week, before Robert Heminworth, the eldest son, died also. He collapsed while taking evening dinner. It was discovered later that he had eaten poisoned venison."

"Did Lady Heminworth consume any of the same meat?"

"Yes, they ate from the same joint."

"With no ill effects to her?"

"None, but the renewed distress pushed her to the brink of a complete breakdown. The poor state of her nerves is apparent to all who see my aunt. And yet, that is not the worst of it. An apparition of a jester in full costume appeared, calling from the edge of the nearby wood on the evenings when the deaths occurred."

Holmes looked thoughtful and leaned forward in his chair. "Obviously a trick to imply that the curse of Brian Delacroix was responsible. Was any attempt made to approach this apparition?"

"It vanished into the trees on both occasions, as soon as the alarm was raised." Miss Monkton looked from Holmes to me, searching our faces. "But the second time it was pursued by Grover, the gamekeeper. The jester, or whatever it was, fled, but Grover ran so swiftly that he would have caught up, had he not stumbled on a concealed root. On getting to his feet he discovered that he was quite alone, and that there was no sign of disturbance to the foliage around him. Then he saw the apparition again - and this is the hardest part to tell you gentlemen, for it is truly fantastical – a short distance ahead of where he stood. It has since been established that Grover had taken no strong drink that day, or the day before, yet he swears that the jester flew through the treetops. He recovered himself quickly enough to empty both barrels of his shotgun, but the figure did not falter and disappeared before his eyes."

Holmes held up a questioning finger. "Both appearances, you said, were in the evening?"

"Yes, always in the fading light."

"That is certain?"

"Oh yes, so much so that the villagers have taken to calling the jester 'The Demon of the Dusk'. As you might imagine, word of such strange happenings spread quickly."

"It is clear that the person behind this is, or once was, a member of Lady Heminworth's household," Holmes said thoughtfully, "since to find his victims he is able to enter Theobald Grange and move around as freely as he wishes, with some knowledge of its disposition. No doubt this made possible the selective poisoning of Robert Heminworth's venison. It is an old trick, to poison one cut of meat while the other remains unaffected. A common method is to smear one side of the carving knife with the preparation in the form of a colourless paste."

"It is my belief also, that there is a rational explanation." said Miss Monkton. "But my aunt will have none of it. She believes the apparition to be the ghost or spirit of Brian Delacroix, and that it passes through the walls of the house to enter. Nothing will change her mind and, because of her preoccupation with the occult, she is convinced that we are powerless to resist and I have begun to fear for her sanity."

Holmes spent a few moments in silence, oblivious to the clatter of plates and dishes as tables were cleared by hurrying waiters, and to the movement around him as other diners arrived and left.

"I am reluctant to consider a supernatural explanation," he said at last. "Experience has revealed that human hands are invariably at the root of things, however cunningly this is disguised. In this instance however, the disguise is very thin, and there can be no question but that we are dealing with an enemy of flesh and blood. Do spirits have need of dressing gown cords and poison, should they embark upon an evil course? I think not."

"It has proved impossible to convince my aunt of that."

"Nevertheless, this affair has some curious features. You have said, I think, that these murders took place some time ago. As it is only now that you bring them to my attention, I must conclude that you have more to tell us, Miss Monkton, than this account of a medieval spectre. I would speculate that this jester has recently reappeared, to cause Lady Heminworth to fear for her life."

"Your supposition is correct, Mr Holmes. My aunt is plagued by sleeplessness, and is constantly in a highly nervous state. She swears that she was shaken awake by the jester once, in the early hours, but when the servants were roused, they found nothing. His shadow has passed across the walls in front of her, always when she is alone in her sitting room, and there have been more appearances at the edge of the woods. His speech is of the foulest, the sort of language commonly used by the worst sort of person, and he has threatened Lady Heminworth with damnation in this world and the next."

"Again this demonstrates his familiarity with the household. He is aware of your aunt's superstitious beliefs, and is using them against her as a weapon of fear."

"He has warned her that her death is imminent, which can be for no reason other than her distant relationship by marriage to the old de Lorme family. Since my previous visit, which was to attend my cousin's funeral, she has aged beyond her years."

"I sympathise with the lady's predicament, and her distress," said my friend. "Clearly, this matter must be settled before it worsens her condition to the point where serious illness results. One thing I must know before we attempt to resolve it: What action was taken by the police upon the discovery of Sir Joseph's body, and subsequently at the death of your cousin?"

"My uncle's murder was first reported to the police station at Armington Magna," replied Miss Monkton. "Walters, the butler, set off in the brougham about an hour after the body was discovered. This delay resulted from Lady Heminworth's extreme shock and distress, for it took almost that long to restore something of her calm. Upon his arrival, Walters found that Sergeant Grimes

15

had completed his shift and left the station. There is normally little crime thereabouts, and so it takes only two officers to run the place. Constable Peters returned with Walters, and after a cursory inspection of the body gave orders that nothing was to be disturbed in the library and adjoining rooms, which were to be secured. He then borrowed the brougham and drove back to Armington Magna, where he got the postmaster out of bed to send telegrams to Sergeant Grimes and the County Headquarters."

"If only, at that point, I had been consulted." Holmes gave a faint sigh. "Did the constable examine the corridor or hall immediately outside the library door, I assume one entrance only, or the ground beneath the outside windows?"

"I do not believe so. He left quite soon to summon his superiors, as I have described. The following day, however, an Inspector from Scotland Yard arrived by the first London train."

"Ah," Holmes" smile was almost imperceptible. "Do you recall his name?"

"Gregson, I believe. Yes, it was Inspector Gregson."

"Capital. Do you know anything of his conclusions?"

"He said very little, until he had spent some time alone in the library. We could hear him pacing and rattling the shutters for a while, then he came out and questioned everyone in the house. Later, I was able to form the impression that he believed my uncle had disturbed a housebreaker, and the murder was to ensure his silence while the man escaped. Inspector Gregson said that my uncle may have admitted the intruder, since there was no sign of forced entry, and so a local manhunt was begun. Officers were brought in from neighbouring counties to assist, but the search was abandoned after a few days."

"Was anything stolen?"

"Nothing. It was thought that the intruder fled before he could find anything of value."

"But how was the apparition, the jester, explained?"

"It was dismissed as coincidence, irrelevant, or imaginary. Inspector Gregson learned that a travelling carnival had passed within a few miles recently, and he thought it might be something to do with that. I suppose his attitude is understandable, since my aunt's hysteria added, from his point of view, to the improbability of the situation, and he was naturally unfamiliar with the historical background of it all. Others who had seen the jester beforehand kept silent, for fear of appearing foolish."

A look of incredulity passed over Holmes' face. "And what of the murder of Robert Heminworth? How did the police tackle that?"

"On that occasion the gamekeeper, Grover, was sent for the police when he returned from chasing the apparition. Sergeant Grimes telegraphed directly to Scotland Yard at once, before beginning an investigation at Theobald Grange. I understand that this revealed little, but a different Inspector arrived some hours later to take charge." Miss Monkton paused and smiled briefly. "To anticipate your next question, Mr Holmes, I do remember his name. It was Lestrade."

At this, Holmes could not contain himself. "So, Gregson and Lestrade are involved! Two of Scotland Yard's most brilliant detectives, or so it is said. Miss Monkton, do tell us how much light Inspector Lestrade was able to throw upon this mystery."

"I heard that he had attempted to contact Inspector Gregson, who was working on a case in Edinburgh, but was unsuccessful. He examined the Great Hall, where my cousin died, but was extraordinarily unforthcoming as to his conclusions. He did, however, comment unfavourably many times on the previous investigation, that of my uncle's death, before spending some time wandering about the house lost in his thoughts. He seemed to arrive at an abrupt conclusion and went straight to the kitchen, where he conducted a long interview with Mrs Meeson, the cook. A good deal of shouting was heard, and there followed a shorter conversation with Walters, who said afterwards that he had fully

17

expected to be spending the night in the cells of Armington Magna police station."

Holmes laughed merrily at this. "Excuse me, Miss Monkton. I do not wish to make light of your troubles, but Lestrade's path and mine have crossed before. I shall be surprised if we cannot improve upon his methods."

"Then you will accept the case?" She asked eagerly.

"You may depend upon it. There are a few small enquiries that must be made before I can take any action, but they will not take long." He drew his watch from his waistcoat pocket. "But I see that time has marched on as we have been speaking. Perhaps then, we could find a four-wheeler to take you to your hotel. After a good night's rest, if you would do us the honour of calling at our rooms in Baker Street at, shall we say, two o'clock tomorrow, we shall be pleased to receive you."

"There is one thing about this affair that I find most puzzling," I said as the hansom carrying Miss Monkton turned a corner and passed out of our sight.

"Just one, Watson?" Holmes raised his stick and a passing cabby reined in his horse.

"I meant one thing in particular."

"And what is that?"

I climbed after him, into the hansom. "I cannot understand why Miss Monkton told us the unrelated tale of her other cousin, the one who was banished to Australia."

"Possibly it had entered her mind that he could somehow be connected with these tragedies. If that is so, then she is looking to us to disprove that notion, as well as to remove this shadow from Lady Heminworth's life."

"And do you intend to attempt this?"

"Most probably." He paused to call out our address to the cabby. "Can you arrange to accompany me to Warwickshire, Watson?"

"Easily. I would have been offended if you had not asked."

The remainder of the journey was uneventful, with Holmes resting his head upon his chest in silent concentration. In our rooms, he put aside his violin after only a short recital, then we sat around the fire smoking and saying little. I could sense his restless nature forcing his analytical powers into play, and long after I had gone to bed he paced our sitting room endlessly.

I rose just before the clock struck eight the following morning, and listened for sounds of movement around me as I shaved and dressed. There were none, so it came as no surprise to emerge from my bedroom to an empty sitting room.

The remains of Holmes' breakfast lay across half the table. I saw that he had consumed a large meal, which usually meant that he would eat little else for the rest of the day, of ham and eggs and curried fowl. Sitting in my accustomed seat I found that the teapot had cooled, indicating that he had been gone for some time. His discarded early-morning pipe, used to smoke yesterday's dottles, lay balanced on the edge of his plate, and the aroma of tobacco hung thickly in the air. He had smoked heavily, probably before eating, as he sometimes did when contemplating a case that had been laid before him. I looked around for a note, such as he might leave to give me instructions to meet him elsewhere, but found none.

I rang for Mrs Hudson, who brought my breakfast and confirmed that Holmes had left at least an hour before. "I know you're only staying for a short while, doctor," said she, "but it's nice to have you here while your wife's away. It's just like it used to be."

I thanked her and gave some thought to this curious affair as I ate. Holmes had not enlarged greatly on his answer to my question about Donald Heminworth's connection with the rest of

19

Miss Monkton's story, but it struck me that here, also, there were several things to be cleared up. To begin with, the arrival from South Africa had been sudden, with no letter or telegram sent ahead to prepare the family after such a long absence. Then there was the unknown and disgraceful act that had so enraged Sir Joseph, normally an affectionate family man, to the point where he banished his second son to the far-off lands of Australia. A return to familiar territory, to South Africa, would surely have been more bearable to the young man.

I pondered these enigmas that, I had become convinced, were part of the larger mystery confronting us. From the clock on the mantel shelf, I saw that the hour was later than I had thought, so with a shouted word to Mrs Hudson, I left Baker Street for my practice, where I spent a busy morning.

By mid-day I had cleared my surgery and arranged for an eager young locum to come in for a few days, should this prove to be necessary. I returned to Baker Street to find Holmes still absent, and was finishing the light lunch that Mrs Hudson provided when the front door closed loudly and I heard my friend's quick, light tread on the stairs.

"Ah, Watson," he said cheerfully on entering the room, "I trust you enjoyed your lunch. As for me, a cup of strong coffee will suffice. Pray ring for Mrs Hudson while I get out of my hat and coat."

That good lady then entered before I could pull the bell-cord, carrying a tray of fresh coffee. Not for the first time I felt some astonishment at her accurate anticipation of Holmes" timing and eating habits.

When he had sat down and refreshed himself, I asked about the success of his enquiries.

"I first visited an old acquaintance, an expert on heraldry, ancient bloodlines and the like," he said in a voice of restrained excitement. "From there I went to the Reference Library of the British Museum. A short study of the archives revealed enough for me to safely say that I now know enough about Theobald Grange to enable us to begin our investigation into this strange business surrounding it."

I glanced at the clock. "As there remains fully twenty minutes to Miss Monkton's arrival, perhaps you would care to enlighten me?"

"Very well, Watson." His words ceased abruptly as a carriage rattled to a halt outside.

"Another client, perhaps," I anticipated.

Mrs Hudson must have been passing the front door, for it was opened before our visitor could knock.

Holmes sat still for a moment, his head slightly inclined, then he turned towards the door and shouted. "Some coffee for Miss Monkton, if you please, Mrs Hudson!"

"How can you be certain it is she, Holmes?" I asked him. "There is no view down into the street from where you sit, and I could hear nothing of what passed between our visitor and Mrs Hudson."

"My dear Watson," his tone revealed his amusement at confounding me, "there is no mystery about it. When I hear quick footfalls on the stair I know that someone of no great age is approaching, and when that is accompanied by a rustle of skirts, it is certain to be a lady."

"But you were in no doubt as to the identity of the lady."

"I had forewarned Mrs Hudson to expect Miss Monkton's arrival, describing our client to her. Had some other lady confronted her, our good housekeeper would have asked her business before enquiring whether we were prepared to receive another visitor, rather than allowing her to come up immediately."

The light knock on our door prevented me from remarking upon Holmes" reasoning. He called for our visitor to enter and Miss

Monkton came in. We exchanged greetings and she apologised for her early arrival, taking the chair that I held ready. Today, she wore an elegant costume of emerald green, its collar trimmed with fur. Her hair, every bit as black and lustrous as I remembered, gleamed as she passed the window.

Mrs Hudson brought more coffee and cleared away the remains of my lunch. Holmes waited until she had departed and Miss Monkton was settled.

"There is more to this affair than I first thought," he announced. "But one thing is now certain, and that is that there are no ghosts here."

"That does not surprise me," she said, "for I do not share my aunt's preoccupation with such beliefs, as you know. Only the jester is inexplicable to me."

"There are costumiers in every town, Miss Monkton. Or else he knows something of tailoring himself."

"No, I meant that it is his flight that cannot be explained. Grover has sworn on our family Bible that he saw the jester take to the air like a bird."

Holmes frowned. "Sometimes what we see is not what we believe we see. We shall doubtlessly discover the explanation, before long."

Miss Monkton's relief was evident. "Then you will accept the case?"

"Lady Heminworth is in agreement?"

"I informed her of my intention to consult you. She is of course still frightened and confused, and I do not believe that she expects to live beyond the end of these strange events, but you gentlemen are welcome at Theobald Grange."

Holmes reached up to the bookshelves and took a telegraph form from the pile he kept there. "Then let us send a message to your aunt, to say that Watson," he glanced at me for confirmation, which I gave with a nod, "and myself will be arriving by the 6.30 train. This means, according to my pocket-watch, that we have less than an hour to prepare, since it leaves Paddington soon after."

Of all that must have passed between Sherlock Holmes and myself during the journey to Warwickshire, I can remember but one brief exchange.

"That fellow will do himself no good if he continues to consume meat in such quantities," he mused as our train passed slowly through a tiny rural station shortly after leaving the suburbs of London.

I looked out of the window as he had, and saw at once the huge figure of a man who swayed unsteadily along the platform, a whole leg of lamb gripped in one hand as he tore at it with yellowed teeth.

"Meat is not the natural food of man," I agreed. "Such an excess cannot therefore be beneficial."

Holmes turned to face me with an amused smile. "I am aware, Watson, that the Scriptures tell us that the Almighty did not add meat to our diet until after the Flood, but are there sound medical reasons to avoid it?"

"Indeed there are. Man possesses a long intestine, which identifies him as the plant-eater he is, or was. Species that are naturally carnivorous have a short intestine and more powerful kidneys to eliminate the resulting uric waste. While meat remains in the body the rotting process begins, and we are not equipped to contain that sort of bacteria without ill effects. You have just seen the outcome of much ignorance and self-neglect, that fellow is likely much younger than he appears. If he continues as he is, he has about ten more years to live, fifteen if he is exceedingly fortunate. His excessive drinking is, of course, no help to him."

"Pray tell me," Holmes' eyes shone with good humour, "how you deduced that the man is a drunkard. I am intrigued by your observations."

"You will not have failed to notice that exceptionally bulbous nose," I replied carefully, "and the discoloured tips of his ears. Both are heavily veined almost to the point of abnormality. However, I doubt if you saw the front of his body, as I did, since he turned towards us only after you had transferred your attention to me."

"You are quite correct. What clue have I missed?"

I strained to keep my voice normal. "The man wore a heavy watch chain on his waistcoat. Even at this distance I could see that the medallion hanging from it was of the kind usually won for prowess at darts or billiards. Show me such a man who does not get thrown out of his local tavern, insensible, every night of the week."

Holmes' expression changed to something very like respect.

"Capital!" he cried. "Not entirely logical but containing a queer sort of sense, and some imagination. Truly, I never get your measure, Watson."

Miss Monkton had elected to travel with us. She had been lulled into a light sleep by the motion of the train, and now wearily opened her eyes.

"Forgive me, gentlemen, I tried to stay awake."

"It is we who should apologise," Holmes said courteously. "I fear that it was our chatter that awakened you."

She looked out at the scene speeding past. "How much longer, do you think, before we reach Armington Magna?"

Holmes consulted his pocket watch. "Precisely fifty-two minutes, since the train is on time. Before that, if you are quite rested, I should like to hear more about your aunt."

And so, for the remainder of the journey, Miss Monkton related to us how, as sometimes happens in families, she had grown so close to Lady Heminworth as to be regarded as her daughter.

There had, in addition, always been a certain resemblance between the two women, the more noticeable since Miss Monkton reached maturity.

At Holmes' suggestion, she elaborated upon her aunt's introduction to the curious ways of the occult, telling of a séance attended by the lady as a young woman, as well as later incidents involving such paraphernalia as Tarot cards, crystal balls and pendulums.

A part of my mind listened, but as if from a distance. Clearly, Holmes' interest in the supernatural derived from its relevance to the case, since I knew him not to be a fanciful man. Soon my eyes had strayed to the changing scene around us, and I saw new leaves that had not long burst from their buds, and the lush fields now restored to their greatest glory. Sheep and cattle fed, unconcerned with our passing, and snatches of woodland came and went. Multitudes of bluebells carpeted the forest floor like a soft mist.

Presently I became aware that the train was losing speed, and Miss Monkton said that we would arrive at Armington Magna station in a few minutes. We were almost at a standstill when Holmes stood up to retrieve our travelling–bags from the rack, relinquishing them to me so that he could carry Miss Monkton's heavier luggage.

From the tiny platform we watched the train leave, a trail of smoke marking its passage, and I gave up our tickets. Holmes strode beneath a brick arch at the side of the building, leading us into a narrow lane, lined with trees. In the station I had noticed no one but the ticket-collector and a few loafers, and wondered if we were to be met. A slightly bent, grey-haired man came towards us, obviously pleased to see Miss Monkton, and I saw that beyond him a double brougham waited.

"Walters!" She exclaimed, greeting him warmly.

"Miss Florence, how good it is to have you back."

Holmes and I were introduced briefly, and Walters showed us to the carriage. I was glad to see, as my friend walked ahead of me, that he continued to appear fully restored after his recent sufferings from overwork and his battle to free himself from the coils of cocaine. Now dressed in a tweed suit and his ulster, with the ear-flapped cloth cap he often wore, he was once more the man whose singular powers had carried us through so many deep mysteries, the solutions of which had hitherto appeared unfathomable.

"How are things at Theobald Grange?" Miss Monkton asked Walters when we were settled in our seats.

The old butler averted his eyes sadly. "There has been another...visitation. I fear for Lady Heminworth's health if this continues."

Miss Monkton's expression was one of fierce determination. "She can take courage now, for these gentlemen have pledged themselves to find the truth of all this and bring her peace."

I heard Walters say, "Before long, please God," as the carriage moved away.

We drove along roads that were really little more than cart tracks, passing several small farms where working men paused to wave to us from the fields. Presently we came upon the village of Armington Magna, which appeared to consist of a few shops, a public house or two and a small Post Office, all dominated by the high steeple of the church at the end of the single straight thoroughfare. Pretty cottages, some covered in ivy, stood on both sides of the road, with the occasional twitch of a curtain the only sign of habitation.

Walters guided the horse past the church and turned off into a lane darkened on each side by tall firs that met high above us like the roof of a tunnel. After a short while these gave way to deserted green fields and the edge of dense forestland.

"A peaceful, beautiful place," I remarked. "It is sad, that such a cloud hangs over the lives of this unfortunate family."

"We will see what can be done," Holmes said thoughtfully, "to set matters straight."

This was the first time, apart from several short exchanges between Miss Monkton and Walters, that any of us had spoken since passing through the village, although I had been observing Holmes' expression in an attempt to define something of his thoughts. He sat solidly upright, now peering ahead as the lane ended and two high gateposts were revealed, built of rough stone and surmounted by entwined dragons and serpents that stared emptily down at us. Iron gates stood open, to admit us to a broad drive that was completely enclosed by bushes of thick laurel.

The horse slackened its pace; perhaps because it knew that its stable was not far away, but we travelled a good quarter of a mile further before we were confronted at last with the home of the Heminworth family.

I saw at once that the house was all but surrounded by a wood of great oaks for which, I vaguely remembered reading, this area is noted. Theobald Grange was built of red brick that was now much worn and discoloured. The central structure was of two storeys, and the heavy entrance doors of studded black wood, amid a number of small, widely spaced windows. From either end, a curving wing projected towards us like, I thought rather fancifully, arms waiting to embrace all who wished to enter. Near one of them a small, crumbling edifice reminded me of Miss Monkton's references to the East Tower. Pillars of smoke rose above the tall chimneys and drifted across the slate roof that, like other parts of the building, showed evidence of neglect, and I recalled also her mention of the family's deteriorated financial position.

As we drew nearer, a miserable desolation overcame me. I felt a curious deadness of spirit that I am scarcely able to describe, gone in a moment but leaving an impression of fearful anticipation. After the outbuildings, we circled the lawn to reach the gravel courtyard, and I pulled my travelling-cloak more tightly around me.

Walters brought the carriage to a halt and at once a man waiting near the entrance stepped forward to hold the horse's head. Holmes alighted and helped Miss Monkton down, then with Walters and myself removed our luggage before the horse was led away.

Passing through them, the doors seemed enormous, like the entrance to a castle built for giants. Walters took our hats and coats from us, then we left our suitcases to be taken to our rooms later and followed him into the Great Hall. My first impression was of a room adorned with ancient weapons and armour, with doors leading off from the left and right and a small minstrel's gallery above. The panelled walls held many portraits, probably ancestral, for the subjects resembled each other and looked to be from various generations past. Crossed flags and sabres hung above the doorways, and at intervals among the paintings.

Directly ahead, an ornate staircase wound to the upper floor, supported by pillars of oak. At its foot, a woman sat sobbing with her head in her hands. She looked up briefly at our approach, and I saw that she must have been strikingly beautiful once. This, unmistakably, was Lady Heminworth.

The young girl beside her wore the uniform of a maid, and was desperately trying to console her mistress. Miss Monkton gave a little cry and flew to her aunt, embracing her warmly.

"You see, Aunt Mary, I have returned quickly."

Lady Heminworth turned a tear-stained face to her. "Dear Florence, has it been three days already?"

"It has been but two. I have kept my promise to return to you at the earliest possible moment. Aunt Mary, you are trembling!" She freed herself gently from the older woman's grip. "But I am forgetting my manners. I have brought with me Mr Sherlock Holmes and Dr Watson. They will discover whatever lies behind all this, never fear."

Lady Heminworth looked at Holmes and myself as if only then aware of our presence. With a brave effort she favoured us with a warm smile that contrasted sharply with the haunted look that I saw in her eyes.

"Gentlemen, you are most welcome here," she said, "although I cannot have such faith in your success as does my niece, for I believe myself beyond hope. Nevertheless, merely to have your support, your presence in my house, will be an immense comfort."

Holmes bowed and spoke carefully, in his most soothing tone. "Lady Heminworth, Dr Watson and I are here to help in any way that we can. It may perhaps raise your expectations to learn that, in our experience, many so-called insoluble situations do, after all, have their answers. You have my assurance that no effort will be spared until your problem is resolved."

"But tell us, what has occurred in my absence that has distressed you so?" Miss Monkton asked before her aunt could reply.

At this reminder, Lady Heminworth paled before us. Her weak smile faded and a tremor passed through her body. I saw that she was making a great effort to retain her composure. Her voice shook as she spoke to the maid.

"Lily, show these gentlemen and Miss Florence what has arrived."

The maid fetched a cardboard box and held it out towards us, removing the lid. "Begging your pardon, gentlemen," she said. "Mr Walters gave me this for her Ladyship before breakfast, but until now it lay forgotten in the kitchen. My mind was occupied with my duties."

"Why," said I, "it is a children's doll."

"Please, permit me." Holmes stepped forward and took the box carefully. Holding it in front of his face, he prodded the doll with a pencil from his pocket, examining it carefully from numerous angles before removing it. "This," he murmured, "was never intended as a plaything."

"It is dressed as a court jester," I saw Lady Heminworth flinch at my description-"but otherwise, apart from the hideous expression painted upon its face, it seems harmless enough."

"Perhaps, but let us investigate a little more deeply." With that Holmes carefully turned it over, to reveal a wooden handle extending an inch or two from the doll's back. He drew his fingers away quickly.

"It is nothing more than a puppet," said Miss Monkton, "mounted on a stick."

"That may be what we are intended to think." Holmes held it away from him. "I believe it to be a bauble, a comic tool used by clowns and jesters in the Middle Ages. They were more commonly fashioned in the likeness of an ass."

Lady Heminworth clasped her hands nervously. "It is meant as a reminder that my death is near," she said in a whisper.

"The intention is to make you believe that, yes. We will get to the root of this, I promise you. But tell me, when and how did this arrive here?"

She raised her head, and I recognised her look as that of a woman at the end of her reason, yet who was desperately trying to summon the last of her courage.

"It was left outside the front doors. Walters discovered it, early this morning."

Holmes nodded his head. "In this state, exactly, or was anything wrapped around the box?"

"Just as you see it."

"It is clear that your worst concerns are groundless," he said to Lady Heminworth, after a moment, "for this effigy was fashioned by human hands, and someone has altered it in order to

31

intensify your fears. No, there are no ghosts, spirits or demons here. The supernatural plays no part in this."

With that, he replaced it in the box which he pushed into a corner on the floor near the door, with instructions that on no account should it be touched.

"How I wish I could be sure of that," her Ladyship said in a small voice. "I feel I can no longer tell where reason ends and madness begins."

Seeing her aunt's anguish, Miss Monkton guided her across the room to one of the soft, high-backed chairs. Holmes threw me a glance, which I understood at once to be an instruction to act, and so I reached for my bag to mix a sedative of laudanum and other medicines, while the maid brought a glass of water. As Lady Heminworth drank the potion I noted that her hair, which must have once been as black and lustrous as that of Miss Monkton, was streaked with grey. I wondered whether this fearful affair had brought this prematurely, as it had reduced her nervous state to its present sorrowful level. Remembering Holmes' methods of observation, I saw that her costume was unusually plain, almost to the point of drabness, and that around her neck she wore some sort of mystical talisman, held by a heavy chain.

"Try to rest, and in a short while the mixture will calm you," I told her when she had drained the glass.

She smiled sadly. "Thank you, doctor, but the dread I live with will not leave me for long. I have come to believe that there can be no peace for me save that of death."

"Do not despair," I advised her gently. "Trust in Sherlock Holmes. He is the man to help you. He has said as much, and I have never known him to fail to honour a pledge. Take heart, and with a little patience, all will be well."

In a short while, her breathing grew less laboured and some of the fear left her. During this time, Holmes had been in conversation with Miss Monkton. This, I surmised, was to distract her as I attended her aunt.

"Watson," he called to me from across the room, "Miss Monkton has suggested that we retire to our rooms to prepare for dinner. Will Lady Heminworth be sufficiently recovered to join us?"

I considered. "A short rest should ensure that she is, but on no account must she be excited further."

"Naturally not," he agreed. "Lady Heminworth, I trust you are no worse after such an unpleasant experience?"

"Dr Watson's medicine has helped."

"I am glad to hear it. Now with your permission we will withdraw to our rooms."

Walters was summoned, and with a little bow he led us up the staircase and along the gallery surmounting it. The polished floor creaked under us as we entered a long corridor extending across the entire front of the house, with rooms along one side and a succession of windows opposite looking down upon the lawn and courtyard.

Holmes stopped abruptly some way down the passage to peer out of a window.

"What use is made of that area of forestland, to our left?" he asked Walters. "Shooting, perhaps?"

"Oh no, sir," said the butler. "Lady Heminworth has allowed no sports on the land since Sir Joseph's death. That is Maybell Wood, where the spectre, the Demon of the Dusk as some are calling him, makes his appearance."

Holmes turned and fixed his penetrating gaze on the man. "You have witnessed this, yourself?"

"Yes sir, and the gamekeeper, as well as her Ladyship."

"So I understand. It is true then, that these appearances always take place at dusk?" He peered out into the failing light. "At this very time, in fact?"

"As far as I have seen and heard, it is always with the going down of the sun."

"But tonight, nothing is happening."

"It is a cloudy evening, sir. I have noticed that such an occurrence seems to require a clear sky."

"You are most observant, but I wonder how significant that is?"

"I really couldn't say, sir."

Holmes" eyes narrowed thoughtfully.

"I am told that it was you who found the box containing the doll," he said then.

"Indeed sir," Walters looked as if he had been accused. "It was on the stone step outside the front doors, this morning."

"Can you remember whether there was rain, during the night?"

"Quite heavy rain, I would think. It had not long ceased when I arose at five o'clock."

"How can you be certain of that?" my friend asked with interest.

"The window panes were still streaked."

"Excellent. Was the box wet or dry?"

The butler frowned. "It was dry, sir. Even though it was completely exposed."

"Then we know it could not have been there all night. For now, it must be stored in some inaccessible place, to await the official police enquiry."

"I will see to it immediately."

"It is best if I do it myself. Quite apart from the effect it had on Lady Heminworth, that doll is highly dangerous. It is miraculous that no injury resulted when it was first unwrapped." Seeing the butler's bewilderment, Holmes explained. "The end of the wooden handle has been sharpened and, I suspect, coated with some poisonous substance. Also, the body of the figure contains metal spikes that have probably been treated similarly, spring-loaded to ensure that they protrude through the surrounding cloth on the application of the slightest pressure. However, with the aid of the fire-tongs, I should be able to store it safely for the time being. Until I am able to do this, pray see that it remains undisturbed."

Walters paled visibly as he realised how narrowly his mistress had avoided a painful, possibly deadly, experience. I fancied I saw a new respect in his face as he showed us to our rooms.

My room was comfortable, with a ceiling of heavy black beams and rather discoloured wall hangings. An ancient four-poster bed stood majestically opposite the window.

I had scarcely enough time to unpack my few things and change my clothes for dinner, before I heard Holmes' sharp knock at my door.

"This is a curious business, Watson," he said as soon as he had entered. "Our unknown adversary is out to drive Lady Heminworth mad, to wear her down so that she loses her mind. He has already demonstrated some singularly merciless characteristics, and it would be unwise to underestimate him. As to his purpose, I confess to being somewhat at a loss until more facts are to hand."

"The strain on her Ladyship's health cannot be allowed to persist," I warned. "It took no more than that doll, although she was unaware of the dangerous nature of it, to bring on the seizure that we witnessed. Her nervous state is as finely balanced as the workings of a watch, and any further agitation must be avoided at all costs."

My friend nodded slowly. "Miss Monkton has told me that the family physician, Dr Prendergast, is himself seriously ill at present, so I have assured her that you will be an admirable substitute while we are here."

"I will do my utmost, of course."

"Stout fellow." Holmes began to fill his old briar.

"I believe Walters was quite shocked with your revelations about the doll."

"I did not exaggerate." He lit a taper from one of the oil lamps, saying nothing more until his pipe was well lit and he had surrounded himself with wreaths of smoke. "I identified the poison on the concealed metal spikes by the peculiar colour it takes on when dried. When a representative of the official force has seen it, I shall suggest that the doll is burned or buried. In no circumstances must anyone attempt to touch it or lift it from the box."

"You realise of course, that Lady Heminworth is not alone in having narrowly escaped injury from holding that thing?"

Holmes laughed. "Good old Watson! Actually, her Ladyship was saved because she left the doll untouched in the box. Her fear preserved her. I withdrew it to extend my examination, only after I was certain of how the mechanism operates."

"We have at least foiled this latest attempt. If only we could discover the reason behind these outrages."

"In a small way, I feel that I have made some progress."

"I confess to seeing little light in any of this."

"You will recall that Miss Monkton mentioned that these manifestations always occur at dusk."

I put on my evening jacket, in front of the mirror. "I believe she did."

"And that the butler confirmed this?"

"That, also."

"So we must begin by asking ourselves why this should be. What is especially favourable for the jester's purpose at this time? It cannot be the poor light, to aid his concealment, for if our apparition prefers darkness he has all night to make his entrance. No, there is something about that precise time that is essential to his requirements."

"Did not Walters say that nothing happens on cloudy evenings?"

"He did. This infers that a visible sunset is necessary, and I must give that some thought. The other indisputable fact that we have learned is that our enemy is familiar with the house and with the superstitious and sensitive nature of Lady Heminworth."

"It did occur to me that he would have less success if his victim were not so inclined."

Holmes blew out a cloud of smoke. "Anyone would fear a repetitive murderer regardless of his outrageous costume, but to some this would add an element of the ridiculous, rather than fear. In Lady Heminworth's case, because of her susceptibility from a long obsession with the occult, the implied association with the Delacroix curse fills her with mortal, but quite illogical, terror."

He put away his pipe and we went downstairs. In the great hall a long table was set for dinner before a blazing log fire, which added to the illumination from the gas chandeliers and the oil lamps which had been placed at various points around the room. It was fully dark now, and heavy curtains screened the windows.

Walters stood near the entrance from the kitchen. In turn he held out chairs for Lady Heminworth and Miss Monkton, after which Holmes and I were directed to our seats.

The meal began without delay, and throughout I noticed that Holmes, like myself but possibly for different reasons, watched Lady Heminworth closely. When coffee had been served, he asked her questions about local affairs and the day-to-day running of Theobald Grange. His purpose was clear to me when the conversation was steered to include the staff of the estate, for I had seen before his skilful way of drawing out information on which to base his reasoning.

"I must say that your man Walters copes admirably with his duties for a man of his years," he observed when the butler had withdrawn. "I am assuming that he is your only manservant."

Lady Heminworth put down her coffee cup. "He is, Mr Holmes, but it was not always so. Sir Joseph had his own butler, Martindale, but the poor man died a few years ago in a most unfortunate manner."

"There was an accident, then?"

"I suppose that was what it was, but I have always thought that his death could so easily have been avoided. Like Walters, Martindale was quite elderly, and had served this family for most of his life. When he began to suffer from fainting spells and giddiness, Dr Prendergast insisted that he give up drinking so heavily, or the prescribed medicine would have little effect. Martindale liked port, you see, in rather large quantities, and he continued to visit the Cross and Sceptre whenever he could, despite the warning. His health deteriorated further after he fell in with a man called Crown, a hard-drinking travelling labourer, until he died. He was found one morning in a ditch, drowned in two inches of water. Apparently, he had lain there all night."

"A sad end for such a faithful servant," I said.

"Indeed," agreed Holmes, thoughtfully.

"And so, until Sir Joseph's death, Walters assumed Martindale's duties in addition to his own." Miss Monkton took up the narrative with a look that told me she had discerned the purpose of Holmes' questions. "He seemed glad to do so. The only other staff kept here now, besides the maids, Violet and Lily, are Rawlings the groom and the gamekeeper, Grover."

Lady Heminworth, doubtlessly because of the strain she was suffering, had been showing increasing signs of tiredness. Now she excused herself and retired, leaving us to talk amongst ourselves.

"I perceive that you are set upon a course to eliminate each member of the household from suspicion, Mr Holmes," Miss Monkton said. "Now that my aunt has left us we can talk freely, without risk of causing her further anxiety accidentally."

"We would be wise to avoid that," I told her. "I realised earlier how close she is to an emotional breakdown. Her Ladyship needs complete rest. I strongly recommend that she leave this house to stay with a friend or relative, until her troubles have been resolved."

"No, Watson," Holmes said quickly. "If we are to unravel this tangle, it must be done here. It is already clear to me that there are greater depths involved than I at first saw. If the scene were moved, there is no telling what new strategies our enemy would adopt, whereas we know something of the methods he uses in places familiar to him. It is surely unnecessary to state that we will give Lady Heminworth every protection that we can."

"In any case, my aunt steadfastly refuses to leave." Miss Monkton's tone told me that the issue had been discussed before now, and that her aunt was adamant. "She is much braver than she appears. Gentlemen, I am not unaware of your consideration for her, so I know that you will spare her further distress by asking your questions of me. Where do you choose to begin, Mr Holmes?"

My friend considered. "With the groom, I think."

"Was he the fellow who led away the horse, on our arrival?" I asked.

"I did not notice, but it must have been him or the gamekeeper. As my aunt said, there are no other men on the estate, apart from Walters. How did this man look?"

"Tall, though not quite so much as myself," Holmes said. "His hair was fair and rather unkempt, and his eyes blue."

"Then it was Rawlings, without a doubt, for Grover is shorter, of stocky build and was dark before he lost most of his hair."

"And how long has Rawlings been in your aunt's service?"

"He took up his duties here about six months after Cousin Donald's brief return. I understand that he served in India with his predecessor, McKilroy, on whose recommendation my aunt let him have the position."

"Then McKilroy must have been groom here for a considerable time, in order to have gained the confidence of Lady Heminworth and her husband to the extent that they allowed him to speak for Rawlings."

Miss Monkton thought for a moment. "It must be fifteen years, or more. I remember him from my childhood visits here. My aunt and uncle thought most highly of him. Much of Sir Joseph's discarded clothing that had hardly been worn found its way onto our groom's back. A great deal of trust and affection must have existed, for my aunt to confirm Rawlings' appointment without ever seeing the man, because of McKilroy's assurance."

Holmes" eyes narrowed. "Pray tell me how this most unusual circumstance came about."

The room was silent as she collected her thoughts, but for the creak of the ancient timbers and the faint sigh of the wind.

"As I remember, McKilroy was obliged to return to Aberdeen, to care for his mother who had become gravely ill. He had no other family still living, and no friends who were prepared to undertake the responsibility of a sick woman. To support them

40

both, he had arranged to take on a position with a household not far from his mother's home, so that he could live with her and, being a considerate man, he recommended Rawlings to us so that the inconvenience to my aunt and uncle should be slight. As it happened, Rawlings was unable to present himself for two weeks, but Grover adopted the groom's duties for that time, a situation which pleased neither him nor my aunt."

"Most interesting," Holmes commented. "But did this take place before or after the demise of the unfortunate Martindale?"

"I believe that Martindale died no more than a few months before Rawlings arrived to take up his post as groom."

"And where is Rawlings from, originally?"

"I cannot quite recall. From the south, I think," she said uncertainly. "My aunt would know, or we could ask him."

"No, it would be better to leave that, for the moment."

Holmes sat, as was his habit when thinking, with his chin upon his chest. I believe that Miss Monkton thought him to have fallen asleep, for she looked at me across the table in a questioning manner, which I answered with what I hoped was a reassuring smile. Abruptly, Holmes emerged from his reverie and continued.

"Very well, that is quite clear. Now, if you please, we will turn our attention to the gamekeeper."

"Grover," she recalled as she poured herself more coffee, which Holmes and I declined, "was brought to Theobald Grange by Sir Joseph. This, to answer what might possibly be your next question, was a year or two before Cousin Donald's visit. Previously, the post had been filled by a succession of men from the village, none of whom stayed for very long. I know little of him, save that he seems competent in his work, and that my aunt and uncle had no complaints against him that I know of. I do remember a few words of conversation that I accidentally overheard once, between my uncle and Sergeant Grimes."

"Pray enlighten us," said Holmes.

"It was during one of my holiday visits here that I found myself in the corner of the library choosing a book. Some of the shelves are positioned so that they cannot be seen from the entrance, and so when the two men came in they were unaware of my presence. They spoke for no more than a few moments, but the sergeant warned my uncle to exercise caution after taking into his employment a man recently released from prison. Sir Joseph replied that he knew of Grover's past as a convict, but had decided to give the man a chance. After Sergeant Grimes remarked that he hoped such generosity would never be regretted, my uncle thanked him for the information and I heard the door close behind them. I have never mentioned the incident to anyone until now."

"Has the gamekeeper ever made reference to his past?" I asked.

She considered. "Once, as I brought back one of the horses after a canter, I came upon Grover near the stables. He was describing his seafaring experiences to Rawlings, but upon seeing me he fell silent. So you see, were it not for things overheard in the library, I would have thought of the gamekeeper as a man of naval background."

"Possibly he intended to conceal his real past," Holmes surmised, "or perhaps both accounts are true. Do you know of any friends he has in the village? Does he, for example, spend any of his off-duty time in the local tavern?"

Miss Monkton gave a little shake of her head. "I have rarely seen him leave the estate, nor heard of him doing so."

My friend smiled. "This is a man satisfied with his own company." He stood up and I did the same. "But now I see that we have kept you from your bed for quite long enough, Miss Monkton, as you are finding it difficult to keep your eyes open. I would be obliged if you would tell Walters not to lock up yet, as Dr Watson and I will take a turn around the house before retiring."

The butler appeared in response to her summons, and soon fetched our hats and coats. Holmes went over to the corner of the room and retrieved the cardboard box. We bade Miss Monkton goodnight and she ascended the staircase as Walters showed us out into the night.

We stood in the shadow of the house as the doors closed behind us. At first there was silence, but we soon became aware of the low moan of the wind and the occasional cry of a disturbed bird. In a sky filled with scudding clouds, bright stars were revealed and quickly obscured again as was the moon, which shone with a faint and baleful light.

Holmes said nothing until we were past the first corner, well beyond the hearing of anyone in the house.

"Unless I am gravely in error, Watson, we do not know the half of this affair as yet."

"It is a strange business," I agreed. "On the face of things, Grover seems the most likely suspect."

He shook his head, hardly seen in the poor light. "Remember that it was he who chased the jester into Maybell Wood. If he is involved, then that incident was somehow contrived to avert suspicion, but for that he would require an accomplice."

"Miss Monkton thinks it unlikely that he has friends hereabouts."

"Precisely, although it is possible that he has acquaintances from his prison days. But we must not assume too much without sufficient facts, for that is a capital error as I have expounded many times. It would aid our investigation immeasurably if Lady Heminworth could be induced to reveal the reason for her younger son's banishment, if she knows it, and I would favour an early examination of the parchment from the East Tower."

"Be careful with her Ladyship, Holmes. I cannot over-emphasise the delicate balance of her nervous state. Providing no new demands are made upon her, she should be noticeably improved tomorrow. I intend to observe her closely."

"Splendid. As Miss Monkton correctly observed, her aunt's emotional state will be an obstacle to me. I was hardly able to begin to question her."

I looked at him sharply, sensing his keenness to further the investigation. "Holmes, I must insist that Lady Heminworth is left out of your enquiries for now. Nothing must be done to alarm her. Not being a medical man, you may not fully appreciate the importance of keeping her in a tranquil state. With illnesses involving the mind and the emotions, we are at the very beginning of understanding their causes and treatment and, as a doctor, I could not stand by and allow her to be placed again in the anguish we saw when we arrived."

"My dear Watson," he said with some surprise, "I hope you think a little better of me than that. You saw me curtail my questions this evening on account of her Ladyship's sensitive condition, and I will continue to do so for as long as you tell me. Miss Monkton is, in any case, the best source of information at present, and there are always my own deductions to rely on." His brief smile was just visible to me. "Never fear, old friend, by one way or another, we will get through this."

We had almost completed a circuit of the house. After the corner that lay ahead we would stand before the great doors once more, but Holmes turned away abruptly and I followed him down a garden path that led to an area enclosed within a semi-circle of high bushes. He stood still while he looked around us, exclaiming suddenly as he discovered the place he sought.

"Aha! This way, Watson."

He strode into the shadows and I stayed close behind.

"What are we looking for, out here?"

"No longer, we have found it."

Holmes reached up to explore the space beneath the eaves of a tiny wooden structure, no bigger than a sentry box.

"This is where gardener's tools are stored, surely." I whispered.

"And thus an ideal hiding place for this doll, where it will do no harm and be protected from the elements until the official force requires it."

He pushed the cardboard box as far back under the sloping roof as he could, where no one had any reason to pry.

"How did you know this was here?" I asked him.

Holmes withdrew his arm. "You will recall that our rooms face this way, towards the back of the house. Before darkness fell completely I surveyed the entire garden from my window, knowing that such a storage shed must exist somewhere. There was none to be seen, therefore it had to be in a place that I could not see, and the only concealment was behind these hedges."

"Ingenious," I said half-seriously, shivering in the cold night air.

Our purpose here accomplished, we were about to retrace our steps when he placed a hand on my shoulder.

"A moment, while we are still out of sight and hearing. It may be that I shall have to return to London in a day or two. In that event, I rely on you to protect those two women, at the risk of your own life if necessary."

"You need not have asked. My word on it, as always."

"As I expected. No man could wish for a more reliable friend to stand guard in his absence." I was glad to hear that quality of warmth in his voice that was so exceptional to his nature.

"Thank you, Holmes."

"You have brought your revolver?"

45

"My hand rests upon it in my pocket. I loaded it before we left Baker Street."

"I hope its use will prove unnecessary."

"Holmes?" I retorted before he could move.

"My dear fellow?"

"I think, after all these years, that I understand something of your methods."

"As well as any man alive."

Knowing the contradictions of his nature, I listened for humour or irony in his voice. There was none.

"Then perhaps you will be so good as to enhance my appreciation of them. I am at a loss to see why we ventured out here for our discussion, surely little has been said that needs to be concealed from those in the house?"

There was silence between us while he peered into the darkness, examining what he could of the flowerbeds and shrubs, ornamental trees, intermittent statues and the distant dovecote. After a few minutes, he appeared satisfied that we were still alone.

"As this case progresses, Watson, it may become imperative that our findings are kept to ourselves. For now, we will exercise caution. The reason for coming out here at this time of night was to find a temporary hiding place for the doll, which we have. Also, I wanted to impress the geography of Theobald Grange upon my memory and to ascertain the means of entry used by this jester when he wishes to continue his mischief."

I nodded. "He must have his ways, yet we have seen nothing."

"I discerned five possibilities, during our walk."

"You astonish me!" I cried.

"So you have remarked before, but I admit to some foreknowledge of what we could expect to find. The British Museum Library contains some most illuminating books on the subject of our ancestral homes. Now, if you have had enough of this fine country night air, let us go inside."

I struck the heavy door and Walters opened it at once. When we had entered he slid home the iron bolts and ensured that the latch would not turn. Holmes was busy lighting his pipe as we approached the staircase.

"Excuse me, sir," the butler called to me as we were about to ascend, "but am I to know when to expect the other gentleman?"

"Did Lady Heminworth tell you that there is someone else to come?" Holmes asked him curiously.

Walters hesitated. "Not directly, sir. Before you arrived I was sent to Armington Magna to telegraph Scotland Yard, as we were instructed to do if anything further occurred. The answer said to expect an arrival tomorrow."

"Who is coming, did it say?"

"The telegram mentioned Inspector Lestrade, sir."

The following morning, Holmes made no mention to Lady Heminworth of Lestrade's impending visit. I saw with little surprise that her Ladyship, although more cheerfully disposed, still appeared so drawn as to compel me to recommend a further day, at least, of complete rest. Soon after breakfast she withdrew, and so it fell to Miss Monkton to accompany us to the East Tower where the parchment containing the account of the fate of Brian DeLacroix had been discovered.

"Show me, approximately, the size of the manuscript," Holmes requested when we stood before the ruin.

She held up her hands, some seven inches apart. "I would say it was of about this length, and found within these stairs."

He nodded, and studied the hole in the masonry. "Time has weakened the mortar around this stone step, and so much crumbling has taken place so as to make it impossible to ascertain the original size of the cavity. I find it most puzzling that its contents were so well preserved after so long, since they had only limited protection from the elements."

"Do you think they were placed there more recently then," I asked him, "perhaps as part of some plan to terrify Lady Heminworth?"

"It is a possibility. Nothing more, as yet."

"Then it could have been intended that Walters should discover it," Miss Monkton surmised.

Holmes frowned. "It would be enlightening to hear in detail how that came about."

"So you shall, upon our return to the house," she said.

Holmes stood with his head bowed and his arms folded across his chest, deep in thought. The depressing atmosphere of the

48

East Tower was having its effect upon Miss Monkton, as well as on myself, for her expression betrayed thoughts as dark as my own. This was to be expected, for I could not doubt that the high encircling wall had seen much blood spilt through the centuries. I wondered how many wretched souls had met their end by the sword or axe in this place, after languishing in the dungeons that were now filled with earth beneath our feet. Of the stone staircase that once led to long-vanished battlements, only a few crooked steps remained, and such shelter as the tower afforded covered no more than a few rough sacks of animal feed stacked tightly together.

My friend moved to the arched entrance before returning to the steps, examining the structure from every angle.

"That will be quite sufficient," he said when he was satisfied; "there is nothing more to be learned here."

"Let us return to the house then," Miss Monkton suggested.

"When may I examine the manuscript?"

"It is kept in the library and awaits your inspection."

"Then with your permission, or that of your aunt, I will see it now."

"Not yet, I think, Holmes." I said, because a carriage had pulled up in front of the house. "Our visitor has arrived."

The small, wiry figure of Lestrade stepped down and went inside while his driver settled himself to wait. We remained unseen as we were still some way off, but Holmes watched with interest.

"I wonder what he will make of this," he remarked.

We reached the great hall as Lestrade handed over his hat and coat to Walters. The inspector seemed surprised to see us, and I remembered that he was summoned before Lady Heminworth knew of our intended visit.

"I did not expect to find you here, Mr Holmes," he said. "Dr Watson, too! The young lady I have seen before. How do you do, Miss?"

Miss Monkton smiled politely. "I am well, thank you, inspector. My aunt has been ill, and is resting, but I will see if she has recovered sufficiently to see you."

She made to ascend the staircase, but stopped at once at a word from Holmes. "Go to your aunt by all means, but it is not necessary to disturb her. I will explain to the inspector how things have turned out."

She thanked him and continued up the stairs. Walters, who, I noticed, had been regarding Lestrade with a wary eye, took all our hats and coats and withdrew. I remembered Miss Monkton's account of the previous meeting of the two men, when Lestrade had almost made an arrest.

The inspector looked more bulldog-like than ever, as he moved restlessly around the room. He was used to the streets and alleys of London, but was unaccustomed to the surroundings of the country.

"Between you and I, Mr Holmes," Lestrade said when the three of us stood alone in the Hall, "I have never felt that these silly pranks, men wearing jester's costumes and all that, had anything to do with the murders. Someone is playing jokes, badly timed and in questionable taste I would agree, but nothing more than jokes nevertheless."

"There is little humour in this business, Lestrade, I do assure you," Holmes said. "This is a continuation of the campaign of terror against Lady Heminworth that began with the apparently forgotten murders of her husband and one of her sons."

"Until these crimes are solved, their files at Scotland Yard will remain open," the inspector interrupted indignantly. "But after three months the murderer will have moved on."

"This latest development suggests that he has not."

Lestrade looked around him and laughed when he was sure that we were not being overheard. "Because of some new prank? The telegram mentioned something left on her Ladyship's doorstep that upset her." He lowered his voice. "Listen, Mr Holmes, it was against my better judgement to come here today. My superiors at the Yard would throw the whole business out of the window if it were anyone less than the likes of her Ladyship making the complaint. They have enough ordinary investigations that need taking up. All the criminals in London aren't taking a holiday, you know, while I spend time on this doubtful connection to a couple of three-month-old murders."

"I have already satisfied myself that there is much more to this," Holmes replied quietly. "It is because the murderer knows of Lady Heminworth's weakness for things extraordinary or fantastical that he is acting in what would otherwise be an ineffectual and ridiculous manner."

Lestrade smiled and shook his head. "Really, Mr Holmes, you have come up with some odd cases before, but never like this."

"My aunt is sound asleep, Inspector," Miss Monkton's voice cut in from the staircase, "and so could not have seen you today, in any case."

"I'm sorry, miss." Lestrade looked slightly embarrassed. "I hadn't realised that you were there."

"Evidently." Her eyes blazed, showing strong disapproval of her aunt's troubles being taken so lightly. "Otherwise you would not have spoken so freely, I am sure. I see that you have instructed your driver to wait, so am I to take it that you will not be staying for luncheon?"

"Thank you, Miss, but no." Lestrade was not used to dismissals of this sort, and he showed his discomfort. "I must return to London as soon as I have taken the particulars of what has happened here."

Her spirited glare did not waver. "My aunt has received a strange object, a doll. Perhaps it is hardly worth your attention, as you implied, but Mr Holmes has already examined it, and considers that it holds some significance."

"Perhaps." Lestrade struggled to contain his anger. I would have feared for a girl of lower class who had spoken to him like that. "But I must point out that Mr Holmes, although not without his occasional successes, is not of Scotland Yard, but an amateur."

"An amateur of considerable talent, it seems, since he can see where others cannot."

Holmes, I knew, had been suppressing a strong desire to laugh at his old rival's predicament. Now, he spoke before the exchange could go further.

"I was, in fact, at the point of asking the inspector to accompany me to see this doll and perhaps consider my observations concerning it. He may want to take it back to London with him for further examination."

Lestrade cautiously took his leave of Miss Monkton, and left with Holmes for the garden. I used the opportunity to go with her to her aunt's room, where I found the lady awake but still in a highly nervous state. I recommended that she remain in bed until the evening and administered a smaller dose of the medicine I had prescribed before.

"The good inspector was quite shocked when I explained the unusual functions of that doll," Holmes said upon his return.

"I trust he will handle it carefully until he arrives at Scotland Yard."

"If he fails to, he will not arrive." My friend smiled as he recollected the inspector's surprise. "But the box is sturdy and I have cautioned him against carelessness. Now, if we can have the attentions of Miss Monkton, I think it is time that this parchment was examined."

After a short while, Miss Monkton came to tell us that her aunt had once more sunk into a much-needed sleep. She needed no reminder of Holmes' intentions. "If you will please follow me to the library, gentlemen."

We passed into a room that was much larger than I expected. The polished shelves held hundreds of bound volumes dealing with a multitude of subjects. Light from the tall windows glinted on leather. In the centre of the chamber stood an ornate desk with a reading lamp, with several straight-backed chairs nearby.

Miss Monkton produced a key that unlocked one of the desk drawers. She withdrew a small carved wooden chest and opened it with another key, standing back to allow us an unrestricted view. The manuscript was yellowed and loosely rolled, covered with tiny words in a language that I barely recognised as my own.

"May I remove it?" Holmes asked.

"Please take the greatest care. Some learned friends of my late uncle, who examined it originally, strongly advised that the parchment be unrolled only as far as is necessary to read the text. It is so fragile that it would certainly crumble under any but the lightest of touches."

"I will treat it as if it were a spider's web." Holmes did indeed take extreme care, using his lens to examine the manuscript thoroughly. I stood next to him, staring at the barely discernible words as each was magnified in turn. He read aloud, commenting that the unknown author had written from the point of view of an actual witness to the events described. "Possibly a courtier or friend of Baron Roger de Lorme, definitely French or of French descent, from the manner in which the English of that period is expressed. Most interesting."

The time for luncheon came and went uneventfully. Holmes returned to the library shortly afterwards, and I spent the time talking to Miss Monkton until he emerged. Sometime later

Lady Heminworth appeared, and I was glad to note the evident improvement in her condition.

When she had greeted us and apologised for her absence, she sat down and took coffee. I noticed that she trembled slightly and the quickness of her movements betrayed her anxiety, but her features had lost some of the tension of yesterday, and her eyes were now bright and clear.

We all three expressed relief, and her Ladyship asked about Lestrade's visit, before Walters entered the room and stood waiting for leave to speak.

"Your Ladyship," he said when he had her attention, "there are men outside from the circus troupe that passed through the parish some time ago. They are now making their return journey, and ask your leave to form an encampment on the field beyond the north pasture, if you would be so kind."

"For how long?" She asked.

"Is it advisable, Aunt Mary, at this time?" Miss Monkton cautioned.

"A few days, they promise to be gone by the end of the week."

Her Ladyship considered. "What do you think, Mr Holmes?"

"If you feel they would create no disturbance, perhaps it would be a good thing."

"Very well. Walters, you may tell them that they have my permission, on the condition that no damage or interference with the running of the estate results, and that they leave as promised." She turned to us when the butler had withdrawn. "This is not the first visit we have had from these people. It was once a tradition, begun by my dear husband, that they used our land for short respites from their travels. He loved their bohemian ways."

"Lady Heminworth, can you recall for how many years this went on? For example, was it more than two or three?" Holmes spoke with that glitter in his eyes that I recognised as an indication that he had found something of significance. I suspected that his advice concerning the acceptance of the troupe held a hidden motive.

"Two, perhaps three, I cannot remember exactly. Is that important, Mr Holmes?"

"I am not entirely certain, but you can be sure that the pieces of this puzzle are taking shape, even if I have yet to place them in order. One question I must ask you, and its answer might dispel some of the mystery, concerns your younger son's departure to Australia. Are you prepared to disclose to us the reason for it?"

The room fell utterly silent, and I wondered if Holmes would have been wiser to await an opportunity to be alone with her Ladyship before introducing a subject that must surely be painful to her. I silently questioned his wisdom in reminding her of such an incident, when her emotional state had so recently hung in jeopardy.

"In truth, I cannot." Her gaze was fixed on the polished surface of the table. "Sir Joseph's wish was that I keep silent. It was with the greatest reluctance that he confided even in me, and he did not do so until some time after the event."

"And if your life depended upon it?"

"Perhaps then, if there were no other way."

"I apologise most sincerely for asking," Holmes said. "But it was essential that I should prepare you for the possible necessity of speaking out. You may unknowingly have the key to much that has happened."

Shortly afterwards the women left us, as Lady Heminworth announced her intention of showing her niece the collection of astrological books and impedimenta that she kept in one of the other rooms. Holmes and I declined to join them, as my friend wished to inspect the site where Grover had pursued the jester into Maybell Wood.

"A late afternoon walk will clear our heads, Watson," Holmes said as we put on our coats. "I find that the atmosphere in this house is not very conducive to logical thought. Besides, I perceive that there are aspects of my conversation with Lady Heminworth on which you intend to rebuke me."

He was right, but I said nothing then. We left the house and made off towards the long drive, feeling the chill of the coming evening already setting in. After keeping to the edge of the trees for some small distance, we altered our course towards an ancient oak, a mighty tree with skeletal branches reaching low over the earth as if to pluck something from it.

"According to Miss Monkton," Holmes pointed with the stem of his pipe, "this is the spot where the gamekeeper claims to have discharged both barrels of his shotgun at the fleeing jester. But before we conduct our examination, allow me to clear up the confusion you are experiencing regarding my rather tactless questioning of Lady Heminworth." He smiled at my expression. "Oh, don't look so surprised, my dear fellow, I cannot tell what you are thinking, but I can sometimes recognise what is written on your face. Back at the house just now, the way you stared at me spoke volumes."

"I have seen you exercise more consideration before now, Holmes, towards overwrought women."

He blew out a cloud of smoke and leaned against the tree. "You must know that my apology was meant with heartfelt concern."

"I accept that, but why did you bring up the subject of her younger son at all, especially with her nerves in their present state?"

"Because I believe that it is with him that the roots of her Ladyship's troubles lie. The greatest service that we can perform for her is to bring this affair to its end, and to learn more of Donald

Heminworth is to get closer to achieving that. Miss Monkton suspects this also, and for that reason included his unfortunate story at our first meeting."

"It will be difficult to discover the truth. Consider Lady Heminworth's reluctance to speak, even when you put it to her that to keep silent might endanger her life."

He shrugged his shoulders. "I was certain that my question would remain unanswered, even before it was asked. It was the way she received it that told me that here was something more. Moments ago, you were astonished when I read your intended question from your expression. This does not always lead to a correct conclusion, though it does so more often with women than men."

I looked up through the overhanging boughs at the grey sky, and shook my head. "So, Donald Heminworth's departure was not as it seems, since her Ladyship indicated no scandal, and no family disgrace. The possibilities are diminishing. Holmes, what will you do now?"

"For the moment, we must proceed as best we can." He stood up and knocked out his pipe against a gnarled trunk. "It remains vital that we do our utmost to shield Lady Heminworth from our unknown adversary, as we wait for him to show his hand."

"Perhaps things would be clearer if we could find out why her Ladyship will not confide in us?"

"You astound me, Watson, once again." My friend laughed heartily. "It is you who are a mind-reader, for that is exactly what I was about to propose."

With that he led the way further into the trees, pausing here and there to scrutinize a branch or a patch of moss.

"Here is the place," he produced his lens and began peering at a fragment of scratched bark. "This suggests that Grover told the truth when he claimed to have shot at the jester. These are the impact scars of the pellets, but I can see no sign of blood. From the bore of the weapon and the given distance, the marks appear as I would expect."

Holmes stepped back and looked for a long time at the trees that surrounded us, before conducting a closer examination of their trunks. I noticed that he was especially attentive to areas that sprouted thick branches.

"What do you expect to find there?" I asked after a few minutes.

"There would be grooves, if weight were placed on rope tied around the soft bark. Possibly, traces of soot also."

"Ah, you suspect that the jester's flight was contrived like that. The application of soot, I suppose, would make the rope invisible in the dusk?"

"Perhaps it would have done, but I have disproved it. Nothing like that was used here. If an ordinary man, and that is what we are dealing with, make no mistake, somehow took to the air, then it was in a way that as yet eludes me." He consulted his pocket-watch. "But it gets late. Now that we have seen the place where he performs his tricks, it is time to return to the house."

As we approached Theobald Grange we saw, through the uncurtained windows, Walters lighting the lamps all over the house. Room after room became visible to us, and Lady Heminworth sat in clear sight with Miss Monkton in one of the small rooms leading off the Great Hall.

"Her Ladyship seems much improved," Holmes observed. "I must say, she has shown admirable courage in all this."

"Until now," I agreed. "But the only permanent remedy is to expose the source of her anxieties before they confront her again."

"We shall do that, Watson, never fear."

I looked around us while we waited to be admitted. The dusk had gathered quickly, and the trees behind us could now barely be seen. Only a single bright shaft of sunlight to the west relieved the sombre grey of the darkening sky, and the mournful cry of a bird that we could not see reached our ears and died away.

Inside the house Miss Monkton put a protective arm around her aunt and led her quickly from the room, glancing back into the night like a hunted animal. We turned to look in the same direction and I saw my friend tense like a terrier. Vicious, hateful words floated out of the gloom, and at the edge of Maybell Wood a strange, contorted figure had hobbled into the open. My first thoughts were confused, but Holmes instantly identified it with certainty.

"It is he, Watson. Do you see?"

We watched a grotesque dance begin, as the apparition screamed and leapt about. Its laughter and monstrous threats against Lady Heminworth echoed through the failing light at a hysterical pitch. Its boasts of the murder of her husband and son were expressed in words of the foulest obscenity and abuse. I was reminded of a demon from Hell.

"In God's name, what kind of man is he?" I cried.

"One with more than a touch of the Devil in him," answered my friend, as if he had read my thoughts.

Holmes ran into the darkness like a sprinter. I make a practice of keeping myself in fair condition, but I could barely keep up. I caught a glimpse of a costume patterned with coloured squares.

"Faster, Watson, or we will lose him," Holmes gasped.

I renewed my efforts but we were still too far off. Before us, the jester raged on, shaking his fists and turning somersaults as if controlled by invisible strings like a puppet. Then, as we drew closer, he turned and fled for the shelter of the trees.

Holmes altered his course and put on a burst of speed that I could not match, but I saw that our quarry was still faster. My friend began to lose ground, his energy all but expended, and sounds of exhaustion escaped us both as I caught up. The edge of the wood was near, but I knew that the game was lost.

As we fought for breath I chanced to look back at the house, to see Miss Monkton standing alone at the window with the stillness of a statue, while Holmes and I were reduced to a flagging trot as we entered Maybell Wood.

"Whatever else our adversary is, he is an athlete of some prowess," Holmes said between laboured breaths. "My own abilities are far from inconsiderable, but I doubt if I could equal the speed of his escape if I had just performed the strenuous acrobatic feats that we have just witnessed."

I put out a hand against a tree, to steady myself. "I see now what it is that so alarms Lady Heminworth, considering her disposition. Holmes, he was like a thing possessed. I have seen some of the poor wretches in lunatic asylums behave less alarmingly than that."

"They are more deserving of your sympathy than he, Watson. He cannot have gone far, we may yet catch him."

I thought it unlikely, but Holmes pushed through the branches and plunged into the blackness beyond. I stayed close behind him, weighed down by exhaustion.

"Keep your revolver to hand," my friend whispered.

"It is here." I drew it from my pocket and held it ready.

We stood very still, listening for any sound that would give us direction, but for several minutes the silence was undisturbed. I lowered my gun but remained alert for any movement, until Holmes cried out and pointed into the air.

"There, in the high branches! Quickly, your pistol! Send him a warning shot."

I brought up my revolver, but already I knew it was hopeless. There had been no more than a flash of colour, visible for barely long enough for us to recognise it as a man, before the apparition vanished into thin air. Nevertheless, I had now seen the jester fly, and then disappear, with my own eyes.

"How can this be?" I asked my friend in astonishment. "What we have just seen is impossible."

"Apparently it is not. It was a man that we chased, and yet...." Holmes made his way to the place where the jester vanished. "...there is not so much as a broken twig here, nor any friction marks of any sort." He pondered over this for a few moments before turning away. "Come, let us see how things are at the house."

We set off through the darkness, the lighted windows of Theobald Grange serving us as a beacon when we emerged from the wood. The last trees had been left behind when Holmes" sharp eyes saw something that lay among the tufts of grass, glinting in the poor light. He picked it up carefully.

"A pocket watch," said I as he displayed it in his hand. "Could the jester have dropped it?"

"Perhaps." Holmes dropped the watch in his waistcoat pocket. "We shall see what we can make of it, later."

It was unexpectedly simple. At dinner, after we had ascertained that Miss Monkton's timely action had prevented her aunt from seeing the apparition, we learned from Lady Heminworth the identity of the owner of the watch.

"It is Grover's," she said. "I have often seen him wearing it. Where did you find this, Mr Holmes?"

"Near Maybell Wood. I see that the chain is broken, so he may have dropped it as he went about his duties."

I was relieved to see that he made no reference to the jester's appearance of which, thanks to Miss Monkton's prompt action, her Ladyship was entirely unaware, nor to the actual finding of the gamekeeper's watch. Miss Monkton had told us in private that Walters, the only other witness to the manifestation, had been reminded of the need for silence.

"What will you do now?" She asked Holmes.

"Soon we will seek out Grover and the groom, Rawlings. It is possible that one or other of them could provide information that may be useful."

"I am certain that you will learn little," remarked Lady Heminworth, "but if a visit to the gamekeeper's cottage or the stables will help to end this dreadful business, then please proceed."

After an hour or two of light conversation, consisting mostly of her Ladyship's enquiries about the state of London life and society, the women retired. Holmes and I remained at the dinner table, smoking and discussing such things as interested us both. During a short silence, my thoughts strayed back to Lady Heminworth and the remarkable resilience she had demonstrated. I was convinced that, when her cowardly tormentor was apprehended and all fears of the supernatural dispelled, her recovery from the very brink of a serious nervous collapse would begin.

I have mentioned elsewhere that there were times when my friend's powers seemed to extend to the ability to discern my thoughts, although he would deny this and often explain the logical progression he used to make it appear so. Noticing the hint of a smile at the corners of his mouth as he drew from his smouldering pipe, I recognised that this was such an occasion.

"She is indeed revealed as a woman of rare spirit, Watson," he said as if I had voiced my conclusions about her Ladyship to him.

"I would speculate that she possessed the fiery beauty that her niece has, in her youth," I replied, without making reference to his remarkable ability.

"There you are far more qualified to judge than I."

Holmes, as I have recorded before, had an enduring mistrust of the female sex, and I expected him to expound upon this now. Instead, he sank into a comfortable silence as he finished his last pipe of the day, and we exchanged few further words until we rose to make for our beds.

"Make no mistake;" he said, knocking ash into the fire, "our enemy here is as ruthless as any we have faced. His motives are not yet clear, but they are strong enough to compel him to take two lives at least, and to mercilessly terrorise two women. I regret our failure to capture him, tonight."

"We will put an end to him Holmes, before long."

"There are three possible outcomes to this affair," he murmured. "He will be killed before it is over, or he will hang for his crimes."

"And what is the third possibility?"

My friend gestured with his empty pipe. "That we will fail, and he will kill us and the women."

We were reminded the next morning that winter had not yet fully relinquished its grip upon the land. The night had not faded into daylight before a dank mist, such as sometimes hangs over a calm sea at certain times of the year, settled over Maybell Wood in voluminous clouds.

I had breakfasted with Lady Heminworth and Miss Monkton, who had planned to drive around the estate in the brougham with Walters had the weather been favourable, but as it was they withdrew to another room to read or practice embroidery.

Holmes had declined to eat breakfast, and I found him standing before a window, alternately pacing and staring intently in the direction of Maybell Wood as he drew deeply on his cigarette.

"I hope you enjoyed your kippers, Watson."

He had not turned, and my approach had been silent, but I realised it had been reflected in the damp glass.

"I did. You should have joined us."

"You have surely heard me say before now, that when I am grappling with a case there is little energy to spare for digestion."

"So I have. I spoke to Miss Monkton again, before her Ladyship joined us, about last night. She has already ascertained the whereabouts of Grover and Rawlings at the time we were in the wood."

He looked at me with interest. "Grover was in his cottage of course, while Rawlings was bedding down the horses for the night in the stable. That was to be expected. Both men were alone, no doubt?"

"There is no one to substantiate their claims."

He sighed, looking out again into the mist. "Nevertheless, I would not dispute them."

"It has occurred to me, Holmes," I said in an attempt to rouse him from what promised to be one of his black moods caused by enforced inactivity, "that I could have made a criminal of myself, had I fired on that apparition in the trees."

He raised his eyebrows. "How so, old fellow?"

"Because we have no firm proof that it was he who murdered Lady Heminworth's husband and son, only that he is guilty of conducting a reign of terror against her Ladyship. It is true that he boasted of committing the murders, but I cannot imagine, for example, Lestrade, accepting that as solid evidence. Also, when we encountered the jester he did no more than shout threats and curses and he was, as far as we know, unarmed."

My friend turned to face me with a faintly amused look, but I was never to know what answer he would have given, for Miss Monkton entered the room with a parcel in her arms.

"Walters has just discovered this, no more than a few minutes ago. Like the other, it is addressed to my aunt."

Without a word, Holmes took it from her. He examined the brown paper wrapping and string with his lens, concluding, I think, that it too had been exposed to the elements for some time.

"This was discovered in the same place?"

"Exactly the same."

He nodded. "If we wish to spare Lady Heminworth another nervous attack, I suggest that we keep this from her for the time being. It is almost certain that there is danger in this box, so with your permission I will open it myself."

Some of the colour drained from Miss Monkton's face. "Please do, Mr Holmes," she said uncertainly, "but do not disregard the danger to yourself."

Holmes stripped away the string and paper, to reveal a narrow wooden box. He held it at arm's length and slowly turned it until he had examined every side, before carefully removing the lid. From the short distance we had retreated at his indication, Miss Monkton and I caught a flash of reflected light and something fluttered to the floor near my feet.

"Curious, to find such an instrument so far from the coast," he said, holding the box so that we could see the long brass seaman's telescope within. "But that paper you picked up Watson, is it a note?"

As he placed the box on a small table I unfolded the single sheet, noticing that the writing was in the same thick, blood-like ink as on the outside of the package. "It is indeed."

'I wait for you near the wood. Use this to look for me.'

I passed the note to Miss Monkton and went to the window. Outside, thick mist obscured the landscape. Miss Monkton approached Holmes to give him the note, and he spoke some words of reassurance.

"Holmes!" I cried as the clouds parted to reveal something glowing eerily in the midst of the fog.

He was immediately at my side. "What was it, Watson? What did you see?"

"A shape, I thought, near the trees. Ah! There it is again."

We strained our eyes to see, with Miss Monkton standing at the other end of the window casement, until a patch cleared to show an illuminated figure.

"It is he," Holmes said. "How curious. This is his first appearance at this time of day."

"Then that is what the telescope is meant for," Miss Monkton raised it to her face, "so that my aunt can see him closely. He seeks to break her spirit. He will not do that to me."

I swear that I have never seen Sherlock Holmes move so fast in all the adventures that we have shared.

"No!" he cried, and snatched the instrument from her hand an instant before a gleaming blade sprang from within the cylinder, projecting from the eyepiece no more than a half inch from Miss Monkton's face.

Her terrified scream echoed through the house.

To render the thing harmless, Holmes quickly unscrewed the heavy lens. A powerful steel spring shot out and fell to the floor.

"Great Heavens, Holmes!"

"Calm yourselves," he said quietly. "Miss Monkton, are you unharmed?"

"I am, Mr Holmes, thanks to your swift action. But for you I would be scarred, perhaps blinded."

"This device was indeed intended to maim and terrify," my friend said. "When I saw you about to adjust the focus by turning the lens, I recognised a possible triggering mechanism."

"Thank God that you did." Her face paled and she trembled as she spoke. "If it had been my aunt who received it, as was intended….."

"Let us not dwell upon that," he advised. "The danger is past, at least for the time being."

"Holmes!" The mist parted, and I saw the figure again. "He is still there."

"I see him!" His face took on the keen expression that he wore when he had found a trail to follow. "He has no way of knowing exactly when his victim will operate the device, and he must remain in order to provide the incentive to use it. Probably he feels safe as long as the mist persists."

"I have my revolver, Holmes." I reminded him

"Capital! Miss Monkton, are there any firearms in the house?"

"I believe my uncle kept a shotgun in the study cabinet."

"Then I suggest you instruct Walters to load it, and use it to guard you and your aunt. You will be safer, I think, if you remain like that until Watson and I return."

She did so, and Walters brought our hats and coats with the gun. When they had left to join Lady Heminworth, we waited until the mist thickened into a swirling mass before opening one of the great doors and stepping out.

My first sensations were not unlike plunging into a cold and stagnant pond. The mist surrounded us, inhibiting both our sight and our hearing; our whispered conversation had the flat quality of words spoken in a small, airless room. There was absolute silence and Holmes seemed anxious to maintain this, gesturing that I should make no sound as I made off to the left while he disappeared in the other direction. I quickly realised that the mist was affecting my perception of distance. Twice I almost stumbled into hollows that may have been the entrances to rabbit warrens, and once I caught myself from falling over a thick and twisted root. The ground began to rise, and I struck up the incline until confronted by a large stone that I thought I remembered from before. I left this behind and the shifting clouds soon hid it from sight, so that after a short while I became afraid that I had lost my way. Quite suddenly I found myself on level ground again, and to my immense relief the fiery glow reappeared. The jester waited not far off. I drew my revolver and proceeded cautiously.

Moments later, I stood no more than three or four feet away. A small fire blazed behind it, enhancing the figure's eerie glow. It appeared to be unaware of my presence and I could see no sign of Holmes in the gloom beyond so I resolved to strike now, while the advantage was mine.

"I have you covered with my revolver. If you attempt to escape I shall not hesitate to shoot. Now, turn to face me."

The figure made no move.

"I fear we are a little late, Watson," Holmes said from the shadows, "although we cannot have missed him by much since the fire is well made up."

I let out a slow breath. "Holmes, you startled me."

He laughed shortly. "My apologies, my dear fellow, but you know that I can never resist a touch of melodrama."

My pistol was still pointed at the figure. Holmes strode forward and plucked it from the ground. It was no more than a crude scarecrow, clothed in a jester's costume.

"The shining aura is achieved by the use of phosphorus," I observed.

"We have seen that used before." Holmes tore out the bundles of straw from inside the figure and threw the costume onto the fire after a brief examination.

"I would rather forget that we have."

When all was consumed, he stamped out the last of the flames and we set off to return to the house. Walters had proved a steadfast guardian and there was no incident during our absence, but the relief at our return was evident on the faces of both women. Miss Monkton exchanged glances with us, meaning that she expected a full account of our escapade at a later time, but Holmes did mention to her Ladyship that the figure we had seen this morning was no more supernatural than are the ragged effigies that farmers put in their fields to keep the crows at bay.

Later, my friend and I sat in one of the small drawing rooms, reclining in armchairs with a pot of hot coffee between us.

"The mist has begun to lift," I observed, "but the day will remain overcast. Unless our enemy intends to change his methods, we will see nothing of him this evening."

"Most likely not," Holmes agreed. "However, I have no intention of waiting for his reappearance in order to make some progress with my enquiries. You may recall my saying at dinner last night that interviews with people close at hand, such as the groom and gamekeeper, would likely be beneficial to our investigation, and as I have just caught a glimpse of Walters taking a stroll in the direction of the outbuildings, it may be a good time for this. I have not yet heard his account of the discovery of the parchment, and if we follow him now it may be possible to question the groom at the same time. A short diversion to examine the area where we encountered the jester last night may reveal something new in the light of day, so we will attend to that first." He got to his feet. "Come, Watson, I anticipate that our work today should prove interesting."

At the window, we watched Walters until he passed out of sight, before collecting our hats and coats to again venture out into the cold morning air. At the place where our enemy had performed his acts of madness, Holmes knelt in grass that was still heavy with dew.

"He has left a clear record of his presence. Do you see, Watson?" Holmes stood up and walked a few yards towards the wood, to where the grass gave way to patches of bare, moist earth. "But, what have we here? Can it be that he has left us such a distinctive set of footprints to work with? What do you make of this?"

I bent to study the marks closely. "Well, the left foot appears normal, while the other leaves an irregular impression. This indicates, I think, a deformity. It appears that we are looking for a cripple or, at least, a man who limps."

"Splendid, Watson, your reasoning is sound. However, further consideration will cause us to wonder how a cripple, who must place most of his weight on his good leg, produces footprints of equal depth. Did you see that he experienced difficulty or awkwardness with his movements, last night?"

"I confess that I did not. The very opposite was true. He flung himself about and jumped and somersaulted. Not once did he falter."

"Exactly so. Watson, this is the start of a false trail. Our enemy is playing with us. This provides us with an additional clue, but also with another problem, since we now have to discover whose footprints these are."

"It could not have been the same man, by some trickery?"

Holmes shook his head. "I think not. We have seen the jester, and so are able to estimate roughly his size and weight. These impressions suggest someone heavier and slightly taller, from their depth and the length of the stride."

My friend spent a few minutes more in an inspection of the surrounding earth, before we moved on to follow in Walters" footsteps.

After several small huts, some of them in ramshackle condition, we came upon a long, low building from which came the neighing and shifting of horses. Near the entrance, Walters was engaged in conversation with a powerfully built man whom I remembered as he who had taken charge of the carriage when we first arrived at Theobald Grange.

The talk ceased abruptly as we approached, and both men turned in our direction.

"These are the gentlemen I spoke of," Walters told the groom. "Mr Sherlock Holmes and Dr Watson."

"Gentlemen." The groom acknowledged us with a courteous nod.

"And this is our groom, Mr Rawlings."

We returned his greeting and Holmes addressed both men.

"You were, I think, speaking of us in connection with the curious events of last evening."

"Indeed we were, sir." Walters replied. "I was just telling Mr Rawlings of your encounter with the Dusk Demon."

"We were unfortunate," said I. "He was too quick for us, but it may turn out differently, on the next occasion."

"I doubt there will be one," Holmes remarked. "It is fear that is his weapon against Lady Heminworth, and I have all but broken that."

"Thank God!" Rawlings exclaimed, and before he could speak further a violent coughing fit shook him, almost bending him double as he gasped for breath.

"My dear fellow!" I went to him to administer what aid I could. "Do not try to hold back, let the spasms run their course and they will disappear. In a few moments you will be able to breathe normally."

"Thank you, Doctor." Rawlings voice was now quite different, due no doubt to his difficulties. "It is not serious, it comes from working with the horses, taking care of them in all weathers."

"Most regrettable," Holmes said. "I trust you will soon be fully recovered."

Soon Rawlings' breathing eased, and he was able to stand at his full height.

"If you are able," my friend said, "perhaps you would be good enough to tell us whether you yourself have seen this apparition. I understand that there have been several appearances."

The groom shook his head. "No, Mr Holmes, I have never laid eyes on any such thing. I live in that house over there, with the walls covered in ivy, which is within sight of the stables and, apart from a trip to the inn in the village now and then, here I stay. I've heard talk among the local men of course, and Mr Walters here tells me of such happenings so that I can look out for anything unusual, but that is all."

"Then, until Walters arrived here this morning, you were unaware of last night's events?"

"That is so."

"Begging your pardon, sir," Walters made a hesitant interruption, "but Mr Rawlings went without sleep for most of last night, to tend a sick mare. I came down from the house several times to bring him cocoa or soup. It is very cold at night, at this time of year."

"That was a most considerate gesture. The mare is improved, I hope?"

Rawlings nodded. "Her worst time is past. She will recover."

"Excellent. Well, I see from my pocket watch that the time for luncheon is getting near, so we will keep you from your work no longer. Walters, Watson and I will walk back with you."

With a word of farewell we left the groom. We walked in silence until the stables were well behind us, and only then did Holmes speak to the butler.

"I have been shown the manuscript that is said to lie at the root of her Ladyship's present troubles. Regardless of that, it is clearly a valuable historical discovery. It was yourself, was it not, who found it in the East Tower?"

"Yes sir," Walters said cautiously, as if he feared an accusation. "That was about six months ago."

Holmes nodded. "But after the death of your colleague, Martindale?"

"Some little time after, as I recall."

"But before the Dusk Demon, as you call him, made his first appearance?"

"Oh, yes sir. They began no more than three months ago."

"At the same time as the murders, then?"

Walters was visibly saddened. "First Sir Joseph, then Mr Robert. I shall never forget those days."

"Thank you," said Holmes. "It is always as well to have the chronology of events confirmed. Pray tell me how it came about that the document was found."

"As I remember, Mr Rawlings and Mr Grover were arranging a quantity of sacks of animal feed under the portion of the East Tower that still provides shelter. As Mr Rawlings came down after completing his work on the first landing he stumbled, and would have fallen had he not found a hand-hold in the stonework. When he regained his balance, he found that a large crack had appeared across one of the stairs, and I saw the parchment nestling in the crevice."

"Did you at once recognise it, for what it was?" Holmes enquired.

"No, sir, for it was covered by some sort of animal skin. When this was removed, we began to realise the importance of the find."

"This covering did not survive, of course?"

"I never saw it again. It may have been burned, or lost."

"How unfortunate. But I see that we are back already, and I am keeping you from your duties. I am obliged to you."

We ate a light luncheon alone, as Lady Heminworth and Miss Monkton had been called for by friends and driven into the village. Holmes reasoned that this would be safe enough by daylight, but I confess to having had my doubts.

"What did you think of the groom?" he asked me as he emptied the coffee pot.

"I was concerned for him at first, but such attacks are common in those prone to bronchial infection."

To my surprise, he laughed. "Did you notice that Rawlings greeted us in quite a different voice to that which he used after his breathing difficulties? He collected himself quickly, I thought."

"You believe that he was malingering?"

"He feigned illness to cover his error, in the hope that this would divert us from realising that he had inadvertently reverted to his original accent."

"Could it be that, for some reason, he is ashamed of his birthplace?"

"I suppose that is just possible," my friend observed thoughtfully. "For now, we will consider the incident to be another ill-fitting piece of this increasingly intriguing puzzle, which we may need to refer to later. If you have fully satisfied your appetite, Watson, we will retrieve our hats and coats and be off. I trust you have no objection to spending the afternoon at the circus?"

"None," I said, mildly surprised, "if we can learn something from such a visit."

And so we set off. I judged that we had walked well over a mile and possibly nearly two, before we passed through the north pasture and entered the field beyond. Soon after, we came upon a small herd of horses grazing freely. Looking for signs of the circus encampment we reached the summit of a low hill, to see before us twenty or more caravans arranged in a rough half-circle. Several stout cages, mounted on wheels, stood together nearby. From the first of these a bedraggled leopard looked out and yawned cavernously, revealing yellowed teeth.

"A sorrowful existence for such proud beasts," Holmes remarked.

We passed the remaining cages in silence, disgusted by the smell and the evident neglect. Apes regarded us with lustreless eyes, and various small creatures watched us in hopelessness and despair. Lions, tigers and a single panther lay listlessly, their spirits eroded by captivity and the whip.

"This is monstrous," I said in answer to my friend. "I have seen these beasts stalking the forests where they were meant to live. It seems an act of great cruelty to remove them."

A number of weathered tents had been pitched close to the caravans. From one of these an urchin, wearing ill-matching clothes that were too large for him, carried a wooden pail. He saw us and was still at once, letting the bucket drop as his eyes grew wide with fearful anticipation.

"Please do not be alarmed," said Holmes. "We wish only to see the master or owner of the circus. Will you tell us which of these is his caravan?"

For a few moments, the boy looked at us suspiciously. "Who shall I say is asking, then?" He said at last.

"Please be good enough to announce us as Mr Sherlock Holmes and Dr Watson."

"You wait there." He ran to the largest caravan and pounded upon the cracked wooden door, shouting something that was understood by neither Holmes nor myself. I heard the tortured creak of hinges left too long without oil, then caught a glimpse of a red-sleeved arm before the boy was pulled quickly inside and the door slammed after him.

"They seem to be a secretive folk, Holmes."

"Cautiousness is to be expected."

Before another word could be said, the caravan door was flung open and the urchin made off. Framed in the doorway stood a hulk of a man, red-faced with a mop of black hair and an untrimmed moustache. He wore a red tunic; reminiscent of a hussar's uniform, and tight dirty jodhpurs. A battered top hat was clutched in one hand.

"Gentlemen!" he greeted us in a voice rich with traces of a multitude of accents. "If it is the animals that concern you, I should mention that their condition is entirely due to the recent death of their trainer, and to a general lack of funds. However their plight is temporary, as we have received a good offer. They will spend their remaining years in a private menagerie."

I hoped their lives would be much improved by this. "The circus is to end, then?" I speculated.

"The circus never ends, sir," he observed philosophically. "Indeed, some say that life itself is a circus. As for us, we go to join a much larger concern that we chanced to meet during our recent tour of Europe. They have not fallen on the hard times that we have, and give performances that have been seen by the crowned heads of four countries."

"Most impressive," Holmes commented. "But tell me sir, how did the audiences in Venice, and more recently those of Russia, receive the entertainment you brought to them?"

The man fell silent at once, and looked at us long and hard. I tightened my grip on the revolver in my pocket for, although middle-aged, he would be a formidable opponent and could summon assistance with a shout or whistle.

Fortunately, my fears were groundless. His brow cleared and he smiled as he approached us, bowing courteously when we faced each other.

"Good sirs," said he, "I am Thaddeus Zamil, ringmaster and owner of this travelling establishment. My apologies, for it is only now that I recognise you from the names the boy gave me. Mr Holmes, I have read of your strange and mysterious cases in London newspapers and periodicals, and marvelled at your powers. You must be the talk of the capital, and I don't know where Scotland Yard would be without your considerable help. I see that Dr Watson is here to serve as your chronicler, as always. You are both welcome."

Holmes inclined his head. "I am obliged, Mr Zamil, but I think Inspector Lestrade would take issue with you regarding the value of my occasional trifling assistance to the official force."

The ringmaster laughed loudly as he led the way into his quarters. Once inside he stopped, looking artfully back at us. "But already you have amazed me. I cannot think how you knew of our travels."

"That is no mystery." Holmes lowered his head as he entered. "You have replaced the metal buttons of your tunic with wooden ones from Venice. I could just make out the emblem on the largest of them; the winged lion is representative of that state although it does not originate there. Now that you stand closer, the carved Italian word "viaggiatore" is also visible."

""Traveller"," he translated in astonishment. "But what of Russia?"

"That icon fixed to your caravan as a decoration is most prominent. I should say that not too much time has passed since you acquired it, or our English weather would have dulled the varnish."

Mr Zamil clapped his hands with good humour. "I am without words to describe such a performance. Such magic!" he cried. "What a fine act you would be in any circus, Mr Holmes, what a fine act!"

Doubtlessly he believed that such a notion would be complimentary to Holmes, but having made a similar mistake early in our association, I knew otherwise. The interior of the caravan was far more spacious than was indicated by its outside dimensions, and we sat cautiously upon worn armchairs placed around a smoking oil stove. The ringmaster seated himself and glanced around until he found a rum bottle which he inclined towards us, but which we refused.

"So, gentlemen," he said, pouring himself half a tumbler of the dark spirit, "pray satisfy my curiosity. What brings you to us?"

"It may be that you can assist me in the capture of a notorious burglar who is at large in this area, if you are willing."

Mr Zamil looked surprised. It occurred to me that he probably expected to be confronted with a case of poaching, or petty theft.

"I would be honoured to help, Mr Holmes, but I do assure you that I would never allow my circus to become a refuge for fugitives from the law."

"Of that I have no doubt, Mr Zamil. My reason for seeking you out will become clear when I explain that this particular housebreaker invariably makes his escape by means of acrobatics. He has been known to somersault from windows, walk a tightrope strung between buildings and swing like a monkey through trees in order to evade his pursuers."

The ringmaster drank from his glass and wiped his mouth on the sleeve of his tunic. "So you come to me because you suspect a circus performer?"

"I consider it more likely that he may have worked in a circus in the past."

"Because, perhaps, he has struck when there is no circus in the area? Oh yes, I see that."

He pushed himself to his feet with some effort, and lumbered to the other end of the caravan, where the wooden walls were emblazoned with colourful posters of past performances. A drawer was pulled open and impatiently slammed shut, and then another. I moved in my chair so that I could see him sorting through a small desk, picking up and discarding handbills and posters until he held one up in triumph. Then he came back and seated himself once more. "Now, gentlemen, I can remember but two with the skills that you describe. There was Tommy Fine, Bofono the Clown he called himself, a capable little fellow who left us from this very site to marry a girl from Warwick. He abandoned his profession to become apprenticed to his father-in-law, a butcher."

"Is that his picture you are holding?" I asked, meaning the vivid sketch among the garish lettering of the poster.

"No, doctor," he bared his uneven teeth in a wide grin. "This is the second possibility; the one I would place my bet on, an act which was our star attraction for a good while. Let me introduce you to Flying Fergus Farraday, Master of the Air."

"A trapeze artist," Holmes observed.

"But he was so much more, sir, so much more. You should have seen him ride a monocycle across a tightrope with a chimpanzee perched on his back. I swear that his act would have been little improved had he sprouted wings. Never known to use a safety net, and never once fell. Not so much as a sprained ankle did he ever suffer, all through his career. A true champion of his skill."

"What befell him, then? Did he retire from his profession?" Holmes enquired.

Mr Zamil shook his head. "We didn't think he'd ever leave because he loved his work, loved the applause, you see. Fergus never married, so the circus was all he had. There was a scandal, a murder here, and the police suspected all of us for a time, until they found there was no evidence against anyone, then they let us go. Shortly after, Fergus disappeared."

Holmes" posture stiffened. "Pray tell us of this," he said.

The ringmaster scratched his unshaven chin, remembering. "As I recall, the whole business remained a mystery to everyone, including the county force. One of the animal trainers, Ivan Barcherov I think his name was, or something like that, had saved a considerable sum from his wages. Everyone in the circus knew about it, because Barcherov had told us he was going to use it to go back to Russia. He never did, because he was found dead in the ring. I should explain that every performer takes his turn to sweep the area and spread new sawdust after each show, and he had just done this late at night. He had been strangled, and his money belt was gone."

"The police reconstructed the whole thing, surely," Holmes said expectantly. "The sawdust would have told them everything."

"I fear they lack your abilities, Mr Holmes." Mr Zamil smiled ruefully. "However, to be fair to them, there was little to indicate what had happened. Apart from Barcherov's, there were no footprints in the fresh sawdust, absolutely none, only a single curving line leading from the big top entrance to Barcherov's body and back again. It looked as if a piece of rope had been dragged across the floor. The police could make nothing of it."

"Most curious. About how long after this did Farraday disappear?"

"I would say no more than a month or two. One morning we all arose from our beds, breakfasted and fed the animals, and were busying ourselves with the small tasks that must be done, before Fergus was missed. This was highly unusual, since his normal practice was to be up with the lark, and so a group of us went immediately to his tent."

"To find it empty?" I anticipated.

"We did, doctor. He'd cleared everything out, not that he had much, and we never saw him again. In the years he'd been with us, no one had got to know him really well, but all the same it was upsetting to those who'd worked with him."

"I'm sure," Holmes agreed. "But tell me, Mr Zamil, how long is it, since Farraday was last seen?"

"A good six years, I think."

"Do you think he left in secret because of the murder?"

"I couldn't really say, but I don't remember that he was suspected, particularly. The only one who was, Abdullah the snake charmer, was soon released."

"Why do you think he was singled out?"

The ringmaster stroked his moustache. "I think it was something to do with the line in the sawdust. The police had some theory about a trained python."

"Who is able to unbuckle a money belt," my friend said with a trace of mirth. "Well trained, indeed."

"I said as much, but I am only a circus performer, as the inspector reminded me."

"I hope you paid him no heed. Did the circus move on soon after?"

"You know how it is with us," the ringmaster nodded. "We cannot remain anywhere for long. A few performances, and we are on the road again."

Holmes got to his feet. "My thanks to you, Mr Zamil. You have aided me considerably."

As we took our leave I noticed that Holmes pressed a sovereign into the man's palm. He muttered his thanks and in a moment we were out of the caravan, making our way back towards the north pasture.

"A colourful character." I remarked.

"He is intolerably neglectful to his animals and has questionable personable habits, but he seems a decent fellow at heart."

"His circus has certainly seen better times. I wonder who killed Barcherov?"

"It was Farraday, of course. Ha! I see that the official force hereabouts is no more imaginative than its counterpart at Scotland Yard."

"I'm afraid I don't follow, Holmes." I said with some embarrassment.

"The marks in the sawdust, Watson. Do you not see how it was done?"

"The County Police thought they were the impression of a snake's body."

"What apparatus makes such an imprint, and so distinctly that something must be tied on behind, to obscure the tracks?"

I shook my head hopelessly.

"Could it not be......a cycle?"

I looked at him in puzzlement, then in an instant all was clear. "Of course, Farraday rode a one-wheeled bicycle."

"A contradiction in terms, but the principle is sound."

"But is it possible, to strangle a man while astride such a vehicle?"

"It becomes likely, when we remember that the far more difficult feat of juggling is sometimes performed like that."

I considered this as we paused briefly to look back.

The camp had looked deserted when we arrived, but now jugglers, clowns, a man on stilts, a fire-eater and a young woman who was strapped to a revolving board while a costumed man threw knives around her, had begun a full dress rehearsal. I saw the boy who led us to the ringmaster's caravan, swinging on a trapeze suspended from a branch of a great elm.

"Do we take up our watches tonight, Holmes?" I asked.

He raised his head to the sky. "I think not, we will see no sunset through those thick clouds, and the temperature has dropped since the morning. Our adversary is unlikely to be seen, in the midst of the cold rain which will fall within the hour."

"You seem very certain of that."

"I am beginning to discern a pattern, and possibly the rudiments of an explanation to these events."

"I presume we came here in the hope of discovering how the jester is able to fly. Did you succeed?"

"To a degree perhaps, but I do not yet have enough pieces of the puzzle to form a working hypothesis. There is much that I must learn this evening, Watson, but the more pleasant task, that of enjoying the company of Lady Heminworth and Miss Monkton after dinner, falls to you."

Later, it came to pass as Holmes had predicted. While we smoked in his room before dinner, icy rain lashed against the windows, and the edge of Maybell Wood was beyond our sight.

"As I thought, there will be no dancing spectre tonight," he said as he knocked out his pipe in the fireplace.

"But how can you be certain?" I asked curiously.

"I am not, as yet. There is still much to be discovered." He hooked his thumbs into his waistcoat pockets. "For example, I suspect the jester appears at dusk because only then can he disappear, but that remains to be proven. We have established that he is familiar with this house and with the Heminworth family, to the extent that he can move around unobserved and knows of her Ladyship's superstitious nature. His motive is unknown, but I remain convinced that it is linked with Donald Heminworth's exile, for which no reason has been revealed to us."

"As to Lady Heminworth's fears, I am of the opinion that they are declining." I assured him. "When you pointed out that there was nothing supernatural about that hideous doll, nor about the methods used in the two murders, it had little effect at first, but her improved state of mind was most apparent the following morning. If she can be brought to her senses about this, our adversary's principal hold on her will diminish, as it will with each black deed that proves to be the work of mortal flesh and blood."

"That, alone, would be an accomplishment well worth the time we have spent here," he mused as he took his evening clothes from the wardrobe. "But, my timepiece tells me that it is almost time for dinner to be served. To your room, Watson, dress and prepare yourself. As for me, I have absorbed enough of this good Warwickshire air to give me an unusually healthy appetite."

Dinner passed with most of the conversation taking the form of an account by Lady Heminworth of her excursion to the village with Miss Monkton, and their subsequent encounters there with various friends. Holmes and I contributed a remark or question here and there as we ate our roast lamb, and my friend surprised me in this, for his attentiveness to their chatter was far from the boredom I had expected him to display.

"With your Ladyship's permission," he said when the cheeseboard had been cleared away, "I would like the use of the library for the evening. To familiarise myself with the history of the area and of this house can only aid my enquiries, and I believe the volumes in your collection have much to tell me."

Lady Heminworth, looking much improved, agreed at once. "The library was more used by my husband than myself, Mr Holmes, but I am certain that you will find what you seek there. Please feel free to treat it as your own, for as long as it pleases you."

Holmes rose, bowed courteously and expressed his thanks before leaving us, closing the library door behind him.

For the remainder of the evening I entertained, or rather was mostly entertained by, the two women. Miss Monkton proved to be knowledgeable about a great variety of subjects, and her aunt also held my interest with recollections of her travels abroad. When I glanced at the great pendulum clock I was surprised to find the hour of midnight approaching, and the ladies had just retired when the library door swung open and my friend reappeared.

When he was seated I asked him whether his studies had brought any new discoveries, but he was in a reticent mood and said little. By the time we had smoked a last pipe together he had evidently collected his thoughts, for the sparkle in his eyes told me that he had indeed learned something.

"Have you found information that will help in solving this matter?" I asked, trying not to let my impatience show. "Some clue in the history of the house, perhaps?"

"History is a very variable factor, you know, Watson," he said absently. "Largely, its truth depends on the eyes through which it is seen."

With that we made our way up the staircase and he would say no more, even when I attempted to press him. In the corridor we paused and looked out through the windows, to where the light from the house dissolved into darkness. Maybell Wood lay somewhere in the blackness beyond.

"I am very tired, Holmes," I said when I was certain that he intended to say nothing more. "I will see you in the morning."

"Good night, Watson."

He stood for a moment longer, absorbed in his thoughts. Then he, too, turned away and we retired to our separate rooms.

The sunlight streaming through my bedroom window woke me early the next morning. As I lay in the unfamiliar bed, there were but two sounds disturbing the otherwise perfect silence. Outside, birds sang gaily as if in welcome to the spring, while in the next room Holmes paced back and forth as he always did when a problem presented difficulties because, as he often put it, there was insufficient data.

I began turning the events of the previous day over in my mind. I considered the uneven footprints; the two voices of Rawlings; Thaddeus Zamil, to whom Holmes had described our adversary simply as "a burglar." I assumed his purpose in this was to disguise our connection with Lady Heminworth, thus preventing the spread of harmful gossip. To all this, I added her Ladyship's continued reluctance to speak of her son's exile, and Holmes' revelation that he had solved part of the mystery.

I could make nothing of it all, but the questions tormented me as I tried to anticipate what this new day would bring. As I climbed from my bed the pacing continued. Holmes, I knew, was already dressed, since the sounds were made by booted feet, and I resolved to join him quickly, so that we could face whatever was to befall us, together.

At breakfast my friend was polite but evasive as to his progress. He was quick to reassure both Lady Heminworth and Miss Monkton that there was now, more than ever, good reason to be confident that our enemy, a cruel and murderous opportunist who had exploited her Ladyship's beliefs to instil terror in her, would not do so for much longer.

"I must confess," she said with some embarrassment, "my foolishness in failing to listen to common sense and, Mr Holmes, to your sound advice."

"It is, after all, human to allow our perspective to be formed by preconceived notions," said he. "But I would be the first to agree that not everything can be understood by man nor grasped by science. However, that is not the case here."

"Thank you for your understanding," she smiled. "The presence of you both has been a great comfort to me."

"To me, also." Miss Monkton added.

"Dr Watson and I have pledged our efforts to this business until all is clear," my friend said seriously. "I beg you to exercise the utmost caution until our enemy has been dealt with. It may be that I shall have to return briefly to London soon, this is essential to my investigation and you have my word that I will be away not a moment longer than is necessary. In that event, Dr Watson will serve as your protector in my absence. He has conducted himself admirably in similar situations before, and can be relied upon as myself."

"Of that I am certain," Lady Heminworth said graciously, "but is there any indication as to who our enemy may be?"

Holmes shook his head. "He is a shadow, and as such will fade entirely when enough light is brought to bear. I learned much from a copy of the parish journal in your library last night, and if my conclusions are correct then we are against someone who is quite without conscience. When I have proof we will act at once, but for now we continue our enquiries." He stood up and bowed to them. "Come, Watson, time is passing and we have much to do."

The house was soon left behind and Holmes, striding swiftly, led us at once into Maybell Wood. At first I assumed that we were to visit again the place of the jester's vanishing, but my friend turned abruptly and we made our way through a dense thicket to emerge upon a well-trodden path.

"So we are to visit Grover's cottage," I concluded.

"I obtained directions from Walters, before breakfast. An interview with the gamekeeper is long overdue, but if he is not there we will look around outside the place to see if anything can be learned."

The path was very uneven and waterlogged in places, and continued for almost a quarter of a mile, often growing narrow before widening out to allow us to walk abreast once more. I hesitated when it led off in three different directions, but Holmes had understood Walters well and he proceeded without pause.

"We have arrived, I think." He came to a sudden halt and pointed to a small stone-built house in the middle of a clearing, overlooked by trees on every side.

We strolled up to the door, which, I could see from afar, was in dire need of a coat of paint. When we were quite near, Holmes spoke to me in a low voice.

"He is in there," he whispered, "and is at pains to conceal something from us."

I had seen nothing. "How can you be certain?"

"That tiny window to the left of the door, although filthy, revealed a face that was pressed against it until a moment ago. Having seen our approach, the face disappeared swiftly, but not to admit us since the door remains closed. The urgency is therefore within, and what else prompts such speedy action at the sight of visitors, save concealment?"

"I can think of nothing that would," I agreed, "unless he is rushing to prepare for our arrival. Making tea, perhaps?"

"We shall see. Knock loudly, while I see if it is possible to see through all this grime."

Holmes peered through the other window as I pounded on the door. We heard movement inside, and muttered curses, before the latch was lifted noisily and the door flung open. A short man, dressed in threadbare tweeds, glared at us, his stocky form and almost hairless head bearing out the description given to us by Miss Monkton.

"What do you want here?" he asked, glaring at us with sullen eyes.

"Allow me to introduce myself, Mr Grover," said my friend pleasantly. "I am Sherlock Holmes, and this is my friend, Dr Watson."

"From the house, I know. What is it you want with me?"

"A few words, probably nothing more."

"What about?" Grover asked suspiciously.

"Come now, you cannot have failed to anticipate that the unusual events of late would eventually attract some attention."

The gamekeeper grew tense and I noticed the bloodless pallor of his face, like that of someone who spends much time indoors. I thought this strange for a man of his profession, until I remembered that he had once been a convict.

"Whatever has happened," he said, "it is not my doing."

"I believed that even before we set out to come here. We are not accusing you."

"What then?" A trembling hand gripped the door handle. "Why have you come?"

"Let me say at once that I am aware of your past, and that you have paid for your crimes. My purpose has no connection with that," Holmes assured him.

"I have broken no laws since, I swear."

"There is no reason to disbelieve you. The matter I am investigating is that of the so-called Dusk Demon, the murderer who threatens Lady Heminworth."

Grover's expression softened considerably, he looked as if his soul had been unburdened. "I can tell you nothing of him. There is no one who has seen his face."

"But I understand that you once discharged both barrels of a shotgun at him, in Maybell Wood?" Holmes persisted.

"That's true, sir, but I missed. I must have, for he never faltered. He flew, I don't know how, through the trees as if I'd not fired at all. It couldn't have happened, but it did."

"Most puzzling," Holmes agreed. "But it is becoming a little chilly out here in the open. Perhaps we could come in and discuss the incident with you?"

"Of course," Grover bowed his head. "Accept my apologies, gentlemen. I have heard of you, Mr Holmes, and I know that you help out the police, so I thought they had sent you after me. No one believes me, but I was wrongly imprisoned, you see, convicted of manslaughter when the deaths were in truth an accident."

"It would not be the first time an innocent man has suffered the fate of the guilty," Holmes said regretfully, "nor that wrongdoers have prospered from their crimes. Our legal system was devised by men, and is therefore imperfect. The official force makes more than its share of errors."

"As an innocent man you have our sympathy, Mr Grover," said I. "But what a great pity that you could not have called upon Mr Holmes for assistance. His intervention has brought about the freedom of many who were accused, and would otherwise have suffered punishment."

"I am sure of that, sir. If only I had known." The gamekeeper allowed us to pass into his cottage. Soon we were seated on kitchen stools, which, together with a rough table and an unmade bed against the wall, appeared to be the entire contents of the single downstairs room.

"I cannot see that there is much to tell," Grover began. "I chased this fellow who was dressed like a jester into the woods, just as you said, on the night of young Mr Heminworth's murder. I confess to not believing that I was pursuing a phantom, I thought that a fantastical tale. Just as I got into the trees I stumbled, then got to my feet and picked up my gun quick as a flash, but he was nowhere to be seen. I waited in bewilderment, trying to make sense out of it all, when he flew like lightning, right across my path and through the branches above. I wondered how he could have climbed up there in such a short time, and in front of my eyes he disappeared, but not before I'd given him both barrels. He should have dropped like a stone but somehow I missed, and twice."

"That I doubt," Holmes said.

"But he didn't fall, and there was no sign of blood. Could it be that he really is a ghost?"

"He is as much flesh and blood as you or I."

The gamekeeper shook his head. "Then I am as confused now as then."

"I, too, am puzzled," Holmes admitted. "Dr Watson and I had a similar experience, quite recently."

Grover stood up, letting his hands fall to his sides in a despondent gesture.

"It's beyond me," he muttered. "I thought I'd understood a lot about nature from living in these woods, but not this. A shotgun blast will bring down anything from a quail to a deer, yet this man in his strange costume is unhurt. This must be the devil's work."

An idea came to me. "Mr Grover, do you know of anyone else who has seen this?"

"I think not," he said after considering for a moment. "Usually no one is to be found in the woods…."

Holmes sensed his hesitation and looked up at once. "What have you remembered?"

"It has just come to me that Simon Blackthorne, a poacher who I've had many a run-in with, swore that he saw a strangely dressed man in the same place, not long before."

"Perhaps at the time of Sir Joseph's murder," I speculated.

"I don't know as I'd put too much faith in his story, for when Blackthorne isn't poaching, he's drinking. That's where you'll find him, if you've a mind to, in one public house or another, down in the village."

Holmes nodded. "Perhaps, for the price of a glass or two of ale, this gentleman will add to our meagre store of knowledge of this curious business." He rose to his feet. "Thank you Mr Grover, Dr Watson and I will take a stroll into the village to see what we can learn."

We were about to take our leave of the gamekeeper when Holmes turned to him, holding up something from his pocket. "This, I think, is yours."

"My pocket watch!" Grover exclaimed. "I had given it up. Wherever did you find it?"

"Near to the site of the jester's last appearance." Holmes returned it to him. "The metal is not tarnished, so you also were recently in that area, were you not?"

Suspicion returned to the gamekeeper's eyes. "It is part of my work to be about the woods," he said defensively. "I am often searching for poachers' snares, thereabouts."

"I would have thought that particular spot too near to the house for poachers, but perhaps you observed some curious footprints there?"

Grover's expression cleared again. "Indeed I did. So that is the place you meant. They were strange marks, one boot and some sort of crutch or a wooden leg. There is no one on the estate, or in the village, who would have left such impressions."

"That is what I thought. Good day, Mr Grover."

"He is not the one, Holmes," I said as we retraced our steps along the path. "His size and weight are not those of the man we chased into the woods."

"I had not expected that they would be," my friend agreed. "Since Miss Monkton's description of him was quite unlike that of the jester, as you say. I would like to know what Grover is hiding, however."

"In that sparse room of his, I cannot think that there are many places to hide anything."

"Quite, but you will recall that I looked through the window while you knocked upon his door?"

"Because you suspected that he was busy hiding something, yes."

"As I watched, he hurriedly concealed whatever it was in a small chest."

I thought back. "There was no chest."

"Grover hid it in the only place possible in that room."

"Under the bed," I concluded after a moment.

"Bravo, Watson! Of course I have no means of knowing whether this affects our investigation, but it would be as well to eliminate the possibility, if we can."

Just then, we came to where the path branched off, and took a different direction that would bring us to Armington Magna. It was a pleasant walk, with many trees adorned with new leaves, while others held a profusion of buds.

"We are to scour the village for this poacher, Simon Blackthorne, then?" I asked.

"He should not be difficult to find if Grover's information is correct," Holmes said as he avoided a low branch. "Also, it may help us to mix with the local populace for a short while, if they are amenable. When ordinary conversation is steered in the right direction, much can be learned."

We fell into a companionable silence which lasted, except for the odd remark, for a mile or so. We walked at an unhurried pace, and I enjoyed the peaceful scene, the windswept softness of the new grass, the singing of the birds, the fresh green bushes and the occasional brief glimpse of a woodland animal, while Holmes appeared oblivious to it all. The path became overhung on both sides by low branches, so that we moved through alternate patches of bright sunlight and shade. Holmes walked with his head sunk upon his chest, and his long fingers clasped behind his back. Several times I made to draw to his attention some wonder of nature, something that struck me as particularly beautiful, but I was reluctant to interrupt his thoughts, as he was clearly absorbed.

"I must confess, Watson," he said at last, "that the problem brought to us by Miss Monkton at Brenner's has proven to be at the centre of a far more intricate web than I could have envisaged, then."

I was about to ask my friend to explain his perception of the affair, when we were startled by a profusion of clanging and rattling approaching us from behind. At this point the path curved so that we could not look back, our line of sight blocked by low boughs which were swept roughly aside as a wild-eyed young man wearing a misshapen bowler and creased clothing bore down on us, pedalling his bicycle like a madman.

I have mentioned elsewhere my frequent astonishment at the extraordinary speed that Holmes could command, and I was no less astounded now. The cyclist had barely appeared before he was upon us, such was his speed, but my friend shot out a hand to push me to safety as he leapt in the opposite direction, clear of the path. Even so, a collision was narrowly averted and the rider, with his teeth bared like an animal's, fixed us with an evil glare as he flashed past.

"Out of my way, confound you!" he cried over his shoulder, pedalling faster still.

"Clumsy ruffian!" I retorted, as we regained our balance. "In the crowded streets of London I expect this, but not here."

Holmes brushed dust from his coat and laughed. "I think he might take more care in future. Look."

As he spoke, the cyclist fell from his machine to land heavily at the side of the path. His bicycle, which had struck a thick root extending from the base of a tree, kept to its course for a few yards before toppling against a bush.

"So much for poor manners, bravado and speed," Holmes said.

"Rough justice," I agreed.

We strolled past a few moments later as the man struggled to his feet, dazed but apparently unhurt. He glowered at us through slightly unfocused eyes.

"A wonderful day for a bicycle ride, don't you think?" My friend remarked loudly enough to be overheard.

"Indeed," I replied in the same tone, "but I should be inclined to take great care along this path, it is probably quite dangerous."

Soon after that we came upon the village. Holmes made straight for the Post Office to despatch a telegram to Lestrade at Scotland Yard and, for reasons not known to me then, one each to Aberdeen and Kent. I recalled Lady Heminworth or Miss Monkton mentioning these places in the course of conversation.

"I expect no reply from Lestrade," he told me when we were once more in the village street, "but it may be that my other telegrams will prompt a response by this evening. I would be obliged if you would receive them for me at Theobald Grange, taking them into your safekeeping and showing no one, even if I fail to return."

"I have already promised as much."

"And, as always, my Watson will not fail me," he smiled. "But see who has overtaken us, without any apparent ill effects."

Further along the street our acquaintance from the woods pedalled at a much reduced rate. A group of young idlers hailed him and he swerved in their direction, dragging his foot along the ground to serve as a brake.

"Of course!" Holmes exclaimed as we passed by on the other side of the street. "The brakes!"

"What about them?"

"He has none."

I glanced at the bicycle, which was now propped against the wall of a confectionary shop, and saw that he was correct. The reason for his observation escaped me, but I saw that the group of hooligans had noticed his interest.

"I hope you are prepared for trouble," I warned him, "for it seems that our cyclist friend has told his cronies about our encounter."

"I see that there are six of them altogether," Holmes said lightly. "Strong young men, no doubt, but you carry a stout stick and I have some experience of boxing, so I expect we will give a good account of ourselves."

Ahead of us stood the public house which, I remembered, was called the "Cross and Sceptre". I heard some shouting from the idlers, but they no longer watched us. Some new amusement had taken their attention, and they did not trouble us after all.

Holmes also had turned his mind to other things. "What do you say, Watson, to a pint of good ale before our walk back to Theobald Grange? We should arrive in time for luncheon."

So it was that we sat outside the inn at a rough unvarnished table to drink, warmed by the midday sunshine. Nearby, an elderly man sat alone, unsuccessfully searching his clothing for tobacco to fill his empty pipe.

"Thank you kindly, sir," he said when Holmes passed his pouch over. "You're a gentleman, and no mistake."

"You should enjoy that, if you like coarse shag."

"I do, sir, I do." The old man struck a match and puffed away with satisfaction. "It's good and strong, as I like it."

Holmes smiled. "Obviously, you are a local man, and that is a London brand of tobacco. I would be surprised to learn that it is unobtainable, here."

The pouch was returned. "It's obtainable; it's just not affordable. I can't work much now, too old, so I has to take whatever I can get."

"Quite. But have you no friends to help you from time to time, among the villagers?"

"That I do, sir, but I ain't the most popular hereabouts. I gets by, though."

"Evidently," my friend observed. "I, by contrast, know almost no one here, but am engaged upon a study of village life. Perhaps you would be good enough to recount some of your experiences that you think may be of interest, and tell me of the strange things that I have heard go on locally. I can promise you a full pouch of that tobacco, if you do."

The old man's eyes narrowed. "What sort of things are you meaning? See here, I ain't a police informer."

"I am not from the police," Holmes reassured him. "But the fact is, I have found out that a prominent London newspaper is planning an article, to tell their readers about these rather odd occurrences around here. I am not one of their reporters, but if I write the story first they may well buy it, to save the expense of sending one of their own people. Is it true that there's a man who has actually seen such things, and might be willing to talk about them?"

"Who might he be? And what strange things, anyway?"

"I believe the man's name is," Holmes leaned back in his chair, hesitating as if struggling to remember, "Simon Blackthorne. He is supposed to have seen a phantom in the woods."

"Simon? Yes, I see. I can't say where he is now, but he'll be sitting where you are, sometime after dark. Works evenings, Simon does, but he always comes here for his ale, afterwards." The wrinkled face brightened. "It's the Dusk Demon you're after, ain't it? Well, Simon knows about him 'cause he got frightened bad. Might be willing to tell you about it though, for a consideration. When you see him, tell him I expect a share for my recommendation. John Cradley's the name."

"I will be sure to," Holmes passed him some coins to buy his tobacco. "Tell me, who is that young man over there among the group, standing by his bicycle? I seem to have seen him before now."

Mr Cradley leaned over the table and peered short-sightedly. "That's Bill Cairns," he said disapprovingly. "As bigger rogue as ever drew breath. The police are well acquainted with him, but he's been smart enough to stay out of prison, so far. I heard he got married and moved to Allswood, about five mile away, but that was a few years ago now. They say he treats his wife and little ones bad. If he gets a drink inside him there's sure to be a fight, that's well-known. I should keep away from him, sir, he's a bad lot."

"That sounds like excellent advice." Holmes finished his drink and we got to our feet. "Thank you for your help, Mr Cradley. Good day to you."

As we made our way back to Theobald Grange, I kept a tight hold on my stick in readiness, should Cairns and his friends decide to follow us. Fortunately, it proved to be an unnecessary precaution.

"You intend to return to London, then?" I asked, remembering Holmes' instructions regarding the expected replies to his telegrams.

"I must," he frowned thoughtfully. "I need Lestrade to obtain information from his foreign counterparts, before I can fully establish the motive behind this affair. I shall also visit the British Museum again, now that I have seen the manuscript."

"Will you not find the poacher, Blackthorne, first?"

"That can wait until my return."

I can recall little else that passed between us before we arrived at the house, but I remember clearly the return of some of Lady Heminworth's nervousness at the news of Holmes departure.

"I suppose you must go?" she asked him when luncheon was over.

"I must, if this mystery is to be cleared up properly. But you have my promise," he assured her, "that I shall return at the very moment that the information I seek is in my hands. I know that the good doctor will serve you well in my absence."

From his Bradshaw, Holmes knew that the London train stopped at Armington Magna in half an hour. Lady Heminworth, her voice unsteady, sent Walters to bring the brougham to the front of the house.

My friend quietly impressed a last reminder on me as he put on his hat and coat. "You must not, in any circumstances, leave the women unattended in this house. Remain close to them, within calling distance, at all times. When you sleep, do so fully clothed, leaving your bedroom door open so that you can respond instantly if summoned. Do not allow yourself to think, because of his outrageous costume, that our enemy is anything less than the cold-blooded and ruthless murderer that he truly is, and keep your revolver near at hand. You have my confidence and trust as always."

I reaffirmed my vow to him, and he said no more. The ladies stood beside me on the steps as he said goodbye to us all, and in moments we were watching the carriage as it swept onto the long drive and out of our sight.

The afternoon passed uneventfully. I spent some time in my room with the door open as Holmes had ordered, dozing and considering the events of the morning. Perhaps this poacher, Blackthorne, could provide some clue to cause all of Holmes' accumulated facts to fit into place. The solving of singular problems and mysteries by means of his peculiar reasoning methods was a thing most dear to him, perhaps his sole purpose in living.

I resolved to spend the time remaining before dinner in the library, where I found some volumes on obscure tropical diseases to interest me. The open doors enabled me to see the ladies, across the corridor in the sewing room busying themselves with embroidery. I glanced often in their direction.

When the hour for dinner drew near, we returned to our rooms to change for the evening. I instructed them to call out at the slightest cause. The table conversation was light, being mostly concerned with those floral species that are common in Cornwall, where Miss Monkton lived, but rare in this part of the country.

After a most splendid meal, we fell silent while awaiting coffee.

"My niece tells me that your association with Mr Holmes has brought you some extraordinary experiences, doctor." Lady Heminworth said unexpectedly.

"It is true that some of his cases have been of a most singular nature."

"I have read that his preference is for the unusual, even the bizarre, when the authorities have given up or treated the matter as being of no consequence." Miss Monkton remarked. "As with our situation here."

"I have seen him cast light where the best of Scotland Yard were bewildered," I smiled. "His methods are quite different from theirs, and he rarely fails. Few have ever bested him, and no one has ever done so twice."

Her Ladyship nodded. "His reasoning then, is exceptionally sound?"

"Always. When facts are scarce he forms a hypothesis. Even then, his accuracy is astounding."

"He sees that which is hidden from others," Miss Monkton said to her aunt. "That is the opinion of Mr Cavendish Stroud, on whose recommendation I consulted Mr Holmes."

As we spoke, Walters served us coffee. Now he lingered uncertainly, awaiting an opportunity to speak.

"Begging your pardon, your Ladyship," he began when she noticed him, "but is it in order to bring to your attention unusual happenings on the estate?"

"Most certainly," his mistress replied. "What has occurred?"

The butler shuffled his feet nervously. "About an hour before dinner, I went down to the stables to ask Mr Rawlings about the sick mare. During our conversation, Mr Grover entered to deliver a letter. Mr Rawlings tore open the envelope as we spoke, and his eyes went wide when he read the message it contained. Then he flew into a furious rage and marched past both of us to a bonfire near the potting sheds, where he threw the letter in with the burning branches and dead leaves. We could see that he had sunk into the blackest of moods, so Mr Grover and I left soon after."

"Did you happen to see the postmark on the envelope?" I asked.

"Yes, Doctor. In his anger, Mr Rawlings first threw the letter to the floor, and it came to rest near where I stood. I noticed that it came from Kent."

"Then the incident is easily explained," Miss Monkton said. "I recall that Rawlings lived there with his family before coming to us."

"So, we have no new mystery, after all," Lady Heminworth decided. "But thank you, Walters, for your alertness."

"Wait, please," I said as Walters was about to leave. "Can you recollect any such letters arriving previously?"

"Once only, sir, but Mr Rawlings was not affected so, then. I just thought his actions peculiar, this time."

"It seems so, on the face of it," I observed. "But it will probably turn out to be nothing. The man evidently has relatives with whom he is not on good terms. Thank you once more for reporting it, and be assured that you did the right thing. I was just saying that Mr Holmes often finds that facts appearing to have little significance, later prove to be of immense value."

But I wondered, as Holmes would have done, whether my interpretation was correct. Could it be, instead, that Grover was blackmailing the groom? Or could the letter have been from an enemy in Rawlings" past? Perhaps it was the ill wishes of a discarded lover who had become embittered. I had to confess to myself that the explanation I had given was but a single possibility, without any certainty in it. Holmes would doubtless reveal the truth behind the incident, when I related it to him on his return.

Later, I sipped brandy as I told the ladies of such of our adventures that I had Holmes' permission to disclose. My purpose here was beyond that of idle gossip, for I sought to reinforce their confidence in my friend. The end of this affair would surely be a further trial for us all, and I was convinced that Holmes would shed much light on it, on his return from London.

Presently, I excused myself for a short while and went to smoke near one of the windows looking out onto Maybell Wood. Enjoying the strong taste of my tobacco, I observed that the evening was fine, although far from clear. It came to me that should the jester make an appearance I was powerless to act, for Holmes had charged me with responsibility for the safety of these two women, and their protection was my first duty.

I peered out into the gathering darkness until my pipe went out. There was no living thing to be seen out there, not near the edge of the wood nor upon the ground between the trees and the house. Presently, I became certain that there would be no spectre to dance before an unwilling audience tonight.

Across the room the ladies had been talking in hushed tones, I think about their memories of Sir Joseph. To my shame, I had become drowsy, so that the sound of Miss Monkton's voice from near at hand startled me.

"Come back to us now, doctor," she said. "You will be more comfortable, nearer the fire."

I may have made some reply but I cannot recall, for it was then that we heard the tortured squeal of a door being forced against hinges long disused. We looked at each other in surprise and then Miss Monkton was pulling impatiently at the bell-rope.

"Walters! Walters!"

The butler appeared, breathless, from the kitchen.

"Where were you," Miss Monkton asked him quickly, "a few moments ago?"

"I was in the kitchen, Miss, cleaning the cutlery."

"Then there is someone else in the house. You heard it, doctor?"

I nodded. "I was about to ask if you knew what it was."

"I thought it came from the wine cellar," Lady Heminworth said with mounting anxiety.

"The stairs leading down there are steep and treacherous, but there is no other way," Walters warned.

Miss Monkton's hand flew to her mouth as we heard the sound again.

I took my revolver from my pocket. "Are all the doors and windows in the house secured?" I asked Walters.

"I attended to it earlier, sir."

I remembered Holmes' search for other entrances that an intruder might use, during our walk around the outside of the house.

"Then take a stout walking-cane and stay with the ladies at the entrance to the downstairs staircase, so that you can call to me to return if I am needed. But first, please bring two lamps."

Lady Heminworth now looked as fearful as on the day of our arrival. "Doctor, the sound was probably no more than the house settling, or the wind," she said unconvincingly.

"Then no harm will come from making certain that nothing is amiss." I checked that my revolver was fully loaded. "But otherwise, something may be discovered towards removing the threat hanging over this house. I am going down there."

We crept with great caution to the head of the stairs leading down from the kitchen. Walters opened an ancient wooden door and pointed into the blackness. "Go carefully, sir."

"Please take care." Lady Heminworth echoed. She looked pale, more so in the lamplight. "The steps are in a poor state of repair, and should have been renewed long ago."

I stepped through the doorway and hesitated, praying that Holmes would approve of my actions. "If anything occurs here, call out at the top of your voices, and I will return at once. This corridor is quite well lit, so you should be warned if anyone approaches."

With that, I took one of the oil lamps from Walters and began to descend. There was an immediate curve, so that the glow behind me was soon diminished. Shadows danced unnervingly around me, and with both hands in use holding the lamp and my revolver, I realised my vulnerability. Nor could I prevent the cobwebs hanging from the walls and ceiling from striking my face or body. The darkness was as dense as my balance was precarious, but my concern was for those I had left, that by doing so I might have placed them in the very danger that I was attempting to forestall.

My progress was slow, the lamp revealing no more than a few feet of what lay ahead. I stopped and listened, hearing nothing, and then the restrained hiss of a breath being expelled reached me from some way off. The distance was difficult to judge; I had already discovered the peculiarly deceptive properties of the cellar walls in the poor light.

After a few minutes had passed in silence, I was half-convinced that my imagination had deluded me. I remained perfectly still and alert, until a cough somewhere in the darkness caused the hairs on my neck to bristle. It was now certain: I was not alone in here!

I realised at once that I had no advantage. To the contrary, the pool of light that my lamp cast would announce my position. I tightened my grip on my revolver and continued, desperately trying to move in silence. My foot found a flat surface with no edge to it, no surrounding space to indicate a further step beneath. By moving the lamp I was able to see that I had reached the cellar floor. A crumbling arch stood only feet away, with an even deeper darkness beyond.

I ventured forward and held the lamp high. Bottles and stone jars in racks glinted in the scant illumination, some half-buried in the dust of many years. A quick movement ahead caused me to raise my pistol, but I stopped short of firing as a rat scuttled across the floor.

Again I listened in the silence, but the unknown intruder had concealed himself and was still. I moved the lamp in a half-circle, revealing more racks arranged in rows. Unconsciously I had held my breath but now I let it go, slowly and silently.

A new possibility struck me. What if it were Holmes concealed in this darkness with me? Perhaps he had returned secretly, or not actually left at all, for reasons of his own. He had employed this strategy before, to observe events whilst remaining unseen.

"Holmes?" I chanced revealing my position, whispering and hoping that I had deduced correctly. I was answered only by a continued silence, as I surveyed what I could of my surroundings with another wide sweep of the lamp.

Something in the shadows moved, startling me. I was frozen by shock as a hideous cry rang through the cellar, and a grotesque face confronted me. I recognised it as a painted mask, for nature at its worst could not have endorsed the ugliness of this figure clothed in a jester's costume. He must have entered here with more noise and difficulty than he anticipated, I thought. Perhaps he was aware of Holmes' absence. I forced myself out of my stupor and into action, as the apparition hurled something that glinted in the meagre light and struck the lamp from my hand. Glass shattered on the stone floor and the cellar was filled with darkness. The smell of wine filled the stale air.

Although I had no recollection of taking cover, my soldier's instincts had come to my rescue and I found myself behind one of the thick pillars that supported the roof. I listened hard for the jester's movements, but the only sound was that of the cooling metal of the lamp. I reflected on my good fortune that the packing straw that surrounded me in bundles had not ignited, for such an inferno would undoubtedly have cut off my escape before I could regain the stairs.

I peered into the blackness, and new hope came with the discovery that my eyes had adjusted somewhat. Carefully, I extended my free arm until I was able to discern two racks before me. I crept along the aisle between them with my revolver ready.

Somewhere, I heard the flare of a match. After a few paces the scream came again, but this time I was ready. The figure had positioned itself before a burning candle, with a wooden keg held aloft in readiness to attack. I fired at once, and the report had the power of cannon fire in that confined space. Echoes repeated the blast again and again, ever fainter until they died among the chambers and pillars of this labyrinth. The keg had fallen to the flagstones, the impact covered by the pistol shot, and now I heard the vicious curses of my enemy. He had concealed himself, but I followed his voice cautiously. Once out of this place, I would dress his wound while Miss Monkton held my pistol and Walters went for the local constable. I allowed myself a moment of pride and triumph, as I imagined Holmes' surprise at finding this affair concluded upon his return, and anticipated with pleasure relating my adventure to him.

But this was not to be! Behind me something hit the floor heavily and the candle went out. I turned with my revolver aimed, to realise too late that the jester must have thrown something into the darkness to divert my attention. Now he made off, apparently unhindered by his wound, in a different direction. Pursuit was difficult without light, and the echoes of his footfalls seemed to come from everywhere at once. I found my way to a wall of uneven brick, where an arched door hung open.

I went through cautiously, my revolver steady as I found myself in a small family chapel. It was clearly disused, for the dust of many years lay everywhere. Moonlight, filtering through tall stained-glass windows, gave scant illumination. I could barely see an enormous cross above the altar and shadowy sculptures of winged angels looking down at me.

Near the lectern the jester crouched like a beast at bay, his mask the more repulsive in these surroundings. I lowered my pistol, for I could not fire in a place of worship, as he fled through an archway which I thought must lead out into the open air. An iron-studded door slammed behind him like a rifle shot, and would not move until I overcame the shattered lock and twisted hinges. I put a foot against the wall and wrenched with all my strength.

The night air felt good in my lungs after the dankness of the wine cellar, but my attention was on Maybell Wood, a darker mass in the distance. Seeing no movement I turned to the other direction, around the west corner of the house, in time to watch an indistinct figure disappear into the night.

The hand holding my revolver fell to my side. Suddenly weary, and with disappointment weighing on me heavily, I turned to return by the way I had come. Now that the chase was over I felt guilty and irresponsible for disobeying Holmes' orders, for Walters could not have put up much of a fight if faced with such an enemy. Something glistened on the ground ahead and I knelt to investigate. I recognised the stickiness of blood. The wound had not been enough to prevent the jester's escape, but on Holmes' return we would know to look for a man with a slight injury among the local populace.

I rose to retrace my steps through the chapel, but a tall figure approached.

"Why, Doctor Watson," said Rawlings, "are you all right?"

"I am not hurt, thank you, but I fear that I have just let a desperate man escape."

"Was it the Dusk Demon that Mr Holmes spoke of?"

"Yes. He is wounded, but not severely." I could see Rawlings more clearly now. "I am surprised to see you here."

"It is not by choice. After the nights awake tending the mare I longed for sleep, but none came. For hours I lay listening to the sounds of the night, until I grew restless and decided to walk around the grounds."

"Perhaps I could prescribe something."

"Thank you doctor, but no," he said with some embarrassment. "I was brought up close to the land you see, and we made our own medicine. We used herbs and the like, and so it would be a hard thing for me to take anything else, now."

"Well, if you should change your mind while we are at the house, I am at your disposal. Goodnight, Mr Rawlings."

As I climbed the steps I reflected that the jester's attack could have been fatal had I not had my revolver at the ready, and resolved to continue to keep it by me constantly until we returned to Baker Street. More than once I stumbled and fell on the treacherous staircase, before at last I saw the brightness of Walters' lamp above me, growing stronger as I progressed. The relief as I stood at the top step once more cannot be described, at the sight of my three companions, unharmed.

"Thank God!" Miss Monkton exclaimed as I stepped out into the kitchen. "We heard gunfire."

"Are you hurt, doctor?" Lady Heminworth asked before I could speak.

"Thank you for your concern, but I am more exhausted than hurt."

My appearance evidently testified to this, for Walters put out a frail arm to steady me. We ascended to the great hall, and Walters left us at once. In a short while I found myself once again before the roaring fire with a glass of brandy in my hand. I quickly recovered myself sufficiently to relate my adventure to the women, all the time anticipating the disapproval I would earn when I repeated it to Holmes.

"I do believe," Miss Monkton remarked when I reached the end of my tale, "that you would certainly have been killed, had you not been armed."

"Perhaps, but I was fortunate."

"But for your bravery, we could all have been murdered," Lady Heminworth acknowledged. "Again, we are in your debt."

Warned by the change in her voice, I studied her Ladyship as the conversation continued. After a while I formed the impression that the events of tonight had caused her to revert almost to the highly nervous state of before. She concealed it well, battling against her inner turmoil whilst bravely maintaining her composure, but my original diagnosis was reinforced: A serious breakdown would result if the cause of her anxieties were not removed.

"It has been an eventful evening," I said finally, "and I see that it is almost midnight. I am very tired and I must write a report for Mr Holmes before I sleep, so with your permission, ladies, we will retire."

On the staircase, I reminded both women of the importance of locking their doors. An uneasy night was spent, reliving my encounter with the jester in fitful dreams between long periods of wakefulness. My ears strained towards the open door to catch any suspicious sound from the women's rooms. I had left my report half-finished.

The next morning I was in the library soon after breakfast, wearily completing my account and recording the extraordinary facts of this affair so that it might be added to the published accounts of

111

Holmes' exploits, with his permission. During all of that miserably dull day, Lady Heminworth and her niece were never far from me, as I was determined that my friend's trust in me should not have been misplaced.

Sherlock Holmes returned to Theobald Grange in time for dinner. This came as something of a surprise, since he had indicated that his stay in London was likely to be longer. We received no telegram to forewarn us, and he managed to hire a local trap to bring him up to the house. I thought his appearance somewhat unkempt, with an angry bruise above his left eye, but he made no reference to this and I hesitated to ask.

"All shall be explained at dinner, Watson," he anticipated with a half-smile. "I am eager to hear of your adventures also, for the excitement of them is clearly written on your face."

"You do not look well, Holmes."

"I think that, apart from the effects of a little rough-and-tumble, I am quite well except for the want of nourishment." He drank some of the tea that Walters had brought. "Since leaving here yesterday, I have found time for no more than a snatched bite at a coffee shop, early this morning."

I reflected on how typical this was of him. When hot on some scent, I knew that he habitually deprived himself of food, sometimes of sleep also, for days at a time.

"Then I suggest that we prepare ourselves for dinner, as the ladies are doing at this moment. They will be delighted at your return."

At dinner, Holmes ate with as much appetite as I have ever seen him display. He would say nothing of his experiences until his second coffee cup stood empty, politely deflecting all my enquiries beforehand.

"And now," he said with the glitter in his eyes that I knew meant he had made some progress towards the solution of the mystery, "I will tell you of my discoveries in this singular affair before you, Watson, tell me of yours."

"How did your injury come about?" Miss Monkton also had noticed his bruised face.

Lady Heminworth shot an impatient glance at her niece. "Please, Mr Holmes, let us begin at the outset."

"Very well." My friend settled himself in his chair. "You will have no interest in my journey by the evening train to Paddington, during which I conducted a retrospective review of all that has happened since the moment I agreed to take this case, nor in the short time I spent near the station observing a man whom I erroneously suspected of following me. After spending a somewhat uncomfortable night, I took a cab to the British Museum, where I kept an appointment with a professor of antiquities whose opinions, after I produced the copied text of the parchment and described its condition in detail, were highly enlightening." He turned to Lady Heminworth. "Without doubt, your Ladyship, the manuscript is a cleverly contrived forgery, though its historical content is partially accurate."

"But how can that be," she asked in a confused voice, "when it was found in the ruins of the East Tower?"

"When I examined it, I was instantly suspicious of its well-preserved condition, and it is now confirmed that the weather of centuries would have long since destroyed a genuine parchment so exposed. Having accepted this, the reason for it could only be to plant the notion of a long-dead, vengeful jester in your mind. Thus your preoccupation with the supernatural intensified your fears, and the callous murders of your husband and one of your sons caused you to take the threats of the costumed apparition to heart. As I have known from the beginning, these incidents were stage-managed like a matinee at the Lyceum, by a man of flesh and blood like any other."

"Still, the jester's ability to fly and disappear remain unexplained," Miss Monkton said quietly.

"As yet, they do," Holmes acknowledged, "but we will understand these things before long. For now, let me continue with my narrative."

"Did you see Lestrade?" I asked.

He nodded. "From the museum, I went straight round to the Yard. Some of Lestrade's usual objections to my methods were overcome, when I told him that the professor confirmed the false nature of the manuscript. I suggested that enquiries might be made to substantiate my impression of certain events here in Warwickshire, and with the answers to his telegrams he began to see the murders differently."

"Then again we are to expect someone from Scotland Yard?" Lady Heminworth frowned with disapproval.

"I have told Lestrade that he will be kept fully informed if he holds back for a day or two."

This surprised me. "Then you have discovered all, Holmes, and have in mind a campaign to put an end to this affair?"

"Almost everything is known to me. I mean to see those responsible hanged."

"Did you say *those* responsible, Mr Holmes?" Miss Monkton retorted before I could speak. "Are there more than one?"

"I fear so." He said no more of that. Despite the anticipation that must have been evident in our expressions, he reverted to his account of his journey. "After leaving Lestrade, I took a hansom back to Paddington in time to board the midday train which eventually returned me to Armington Magna, somewhat refreshed after a short sleep."

"So you did not arrive here directly from the station?" said Lady Heminworth.

"I did not, your Ladyship. In fact, I was able to learn as much on my return as I did in London. First I sought out William

114

Cairns, a slight acquaintance of Watson and myself, in the village. I had formed a hypothesis regarding him, and wished confirmation, but he declined to answer my questions and attacked me when I persisted."

"I know this man's reputation," Miss Monkton said. "It may be that you were fortunate to escape with no more than a bruised face."

"Fortunately, I have some little experience at boxing, and this enabled me to avoid sustaining further damage." Holmes smiled briefly. "Eventually I was able to induce him to answer my questions, though he would not disclose the name of the man behind this affair. I am sure that he knows it, but fear has sealed his lips well."

"And so you hired a trap or dog-cart and came directly here," I ventured.

"There was nothing more to be learned by not doing so," my friend agreed. "On the way I passed Mr Zamil's circus, which has left the area near the north pasture to take to the road once again."

"So you learned something of significance in London, and from this man, Cairns?" Lady Heminworth asked hopefully.

"Much more than I have yet said, Your Ladyship, because the source of some of your torment is close at hand."

Lady Heminworth and Miss Monkton looked at each other with worried faces.

"I have made enquiries regarding the staff here. There will be telegrams from Inspector Lestrade, when all is known."

"Holmes, Rawlings cannot be the jester," I said quickly. "I know this for a fact. He, at least, can be absolved."

He gave me a curious glance. "Pray, tell me."

I related again, with occasional interruptions from the ladies, my adventures in the wine cellar and the chapel, and how I saw the jester escape across the fields before my meeting with Rawlings. Holmes listened attentively, only once allowing his expression to show the disapproval that I dreaded.

"So, you see," I said in conclusion, "Rawlings and the jester cannot be one and the same."

"You are correct in part," he agreed. I felt that I had established at least one definite fact, when he added: "But it is not one man alone who has terrorized this house."

The three of us looked at him in astonishment.

"Two murderers?" I retorted, still somewhat amazed at this prospect. "Is this certain, Holmes?"

"It is, but one is a good deal more cunning than the other, I think."

"What must we do now?" Lady Heminworth was clearly shaken by this news.

Holmes considered for a few moments, adopting the position that I have often seen him use, with his palms together in a prayer-like attitude and his chin resting on his fingertips.

"Until this business is settled, you must see nothing of your staff, save the maid and Walters," he said at last. "That much is vital to achieving our aims. Though I have told you little as yet, your demeanour would at once alert our adversary to our suspicions."

With the ladies, I voiced my agreement to this precaution. At the same moment, something else came to mind.

"Holmes, we still have Simon Blackthorne to investigate."

My friend held up a hand in a gesture of dismay. "How can I apologise for my forgetfulness? I neglected to mention my only other call in Armington Magna, perhaps because it came to nothing.

Sergeant Grimes was most helpful when I enquired about Blackthorne, to the point of sending his fellow officer to search the man's known haunts. Regretfully, the poacher has disappeared as he sometimes does, but I have the sergeant's assurance that we will be notified on his return."

"At that time, perhaps we can learn something from his encounter with the jester, if he will tell us of it," said I.

"I would be interested to hear his story. Probably a half-sovereign will secure it for us." Holmes turned to Lady Heminworth. "Your Ladyship, can you describe the characteristics of the land in the direction where the jester fled from Dr Watson? It may have a bearing on things."

She considered, briefly. "There is nothing in that part of the estate that could hide a fugitive for very long. The area is so wild and uneven, that no attempt has ever been made to cultivate it because of the profusion of natural stone half-buried in the earth. There are small hillocks all over, with groups of sparse trees and two or three small streams."

"A horse could not be ridden there?"

She shook her head. "The animal would surely break a leg."

"So the escape was almost certainly on foot. That is excellent for our purpose. Watson, if we set off first thing in the morning, we may find that some signs remain. Now, once more I see that the hour grows late, and a good night's rest will benefit us all."

Next morning we left the house within five minutes of finishing breakfast. As we walked, Holmes and I spoke of our concern for Lady Heminworth's health, for she had again shown symptoms of a disturbed nervous state and passed a sleepless night.

"You noticed the shrill quality in her speech?" I asked him. "That suggests an imminent return to her former state."

117

"Part of the blame is mine," he declared. "I should not have mentioned my suspicions regarding the closeness of the danger, in her presence."

"Her emotional state rests on a precipice," I admitted regretfully, "but I have given her a mild sedative to restore calm for a while. Miss Monkton is to remain with her as long as the jester is at large."

Near the western corner of the building we paused at the ancient door where I had emerged in pursuit of the jester, and Holmes studied it carefully.

"Halloa! What have we here?" He picked up something from the thick weeds that surrounded the chapel. "This crowbar was evidently discarded after being used to force the lock."

"That must have been more difficult than he expected. The noise alerted us at once."

"No doubt you are right, it is a curious way to enter undetected, otherwise. I may need to examine the chapel, later."

"I will be glad to accompany you."

He nodded silently, and we turned to face the bleak expanse before us.

We covered half a mile of increasingly uneven ground before he spoke again. "Watson, why do you imagine the jester chose to enter Theobald Grange through the wine cellar, at that particular time?"

"To do harm to Lady Heminworth, and possibility her niece also," said I. "Perhaps he grows desperate because of the threat we represent."

"That is a distinct probability," Holmes agreed. "As is the notion that he knew the threat was halved because of my temporary absence. This suggests again that he is able to observe our actions at least some of the time, or has it done by someone close to the estate."

"From the outset, you said this was a deeper business than it seemed."

"Indeed. Ah! This may tell us something."

He stopped by a cluster of flat stones near the edge of the path. Nearby was a ramshackle stile and Holmes walked slowly around it, examining its withered timbers first with his eyes alone and then with his lens. He walked on a further ten or fifteen feet and then called to me.

"Observe the stones, Watson; there are spots of dried blood covering them. The stile too, is marked in several places. As some strands of the old wood are broken off, and smears of blood remain in the hollows that are left, we can deduce that our fugitive held on for support, only to receive long splinters in his flesh. The other marks hereabouts tell us that he already bled quite heavily, I cannot imagine that he got much further without help."

From then on the trail was easily followed, with my friend relating how the wounded jester had paused here, fallen there or left the path, to stray back soon after. It was as if Holmes had watched everything.

Soon the few tufts of sparse grass disappeared entirely, giving way to sandy soil, and the low hillocks that Lady Heminworth had described. It became impossible to walk more than a few paces without my boot striking a projecting stone, or slipping into one of the numerous shallow holes at the risk of a broken ankle.

"Holmes, look!" I cried. We hurried to a large boulder a few yards from the path. Blood was splashed upon it in various places, and a series of spots had dried on the hard ground.

"There!" My friend pointed to where the earth began to fall away. "That cluster of boulders looks large enough to have given him shelter."

In the shadow of the stones, we came to a halt. I drew my revolver as we moved together to the rough circle until he raised a hand. In silence, I stood while he leaned his tall frame into the narrow space between two monoliths, a moment before he turned to me wearing a resigned expression.

"You may as well make sure, Watson, but I believe them to be dead."

I brushed past him, hampered by the confined space. Two men lay in a pool of congealed blood, stiffened by rigor mortis and with their faces frozen in surprise.

"Who are they, Holmes?" I asked when he had circled the bodies and returned to my side. "Is that Cairns?"

"It is. That worthy individual has come to a violent end, which is hardly unexpected. The other is unknown to me, but I would not be at all surprised if he is identified as Blackthorne, our missing poacher."

"So one of these men was the jester, and they killed each other?"

He shook his head. "The jester killed them. It was he who left the trail of blood from the wound which you inflicted, but still he managed to murder twice more."

"None of the blood is theirs?"

"Only that from the stump of Cairns' right arm. The hand has been hacked off at the wrist, probably after death. There is no obvious indication as to how they were killed. Perhaps a cursory examination will reveal something but," he added with a wry smile, "we must be careful not to obscure anything that might be of assistance to the local police."

A short while later I was able to confirm his observation. "There is no mark on either of them, anywhere."

He nodded slowly. "They are dead, I suspect, because they had served their purpose and knew too much. Possibly they were lured here with the promise of some reward."

"Blackthorne, I know, had seen the jester at close quarters and possibly recognised him, but what of Cairns?"

"I had my suspicions, and they are confirmed in part. When the remainder are certain, and we have proof enough to satisfy Lestrade, you shall know also."

"But how were these men killed? I confess to being confounded."

"If you will be so good as to return to Theobald Grange as quickly as you can," he said after a short silence, "I will endeavour to complete my own inspection before you return with a constable."

I set off at once. When I turned to look back I could see only the stones, but Holmes would be busy already within the circle. He would spare no effort in his scrutiny of the positions and clothing of the bodies, and his lens would miss nothing of what the surrounding tracks had to tell. I drove myself hard, despite the complaints of my old Afghan wound, until at last the house came into view.

I had been seen from afar, for it was Miss Monkton who met me at the door and, seeing my exhausted state, accompanied me into the presence of her aunt. Walters was quickly summoned to serve me with brandy, and then despatched to Armington Magna to seek out Sergeant Grimes. The brougham returned within the hour, and as the short rest had dispelled my weariness I set out at once with the sergeant. His efforts were admirable, but his best years were behind him and our progress was slow over the difficult ground. To my amazement, my pocket-watch revealed that almost three hours had elapsed from the time I left Sherlock Holmes, but now as we entered the cluster of stones I saw him at once, standing near the bodies in an attitude of deep thought.

"There has been no disturbance, I merely looked at them after I had taken note of the condition of the surrounding ground," he told the sergeant.

"Thank you, Mr Holmes, but what have you found? Did they kill each other?"

"I can see no sign of it. Their attitude suggests that Blackthorne died first."

"Yesterday you told me you had never seen Blackthorne."

My friend smiled at the sergeant's recognition of this apparent inconsistency. "That is quite true. I was able to identify him because I expected his presence here, and from the snares sticking out of his pocket. With the condition of his palms and finger-nails visible to me, the deduction was not difficult."

"A clever piece of work," Grimes acknowledged a little gruffly. "So, the most elusive poacher in the shire will trouble us no more."

"That, he will not," said I.

Sergeant Grimes tilted back his helmet and scratched his head. "I was thinking the murderer might be from the circus that her Ladyship allows to camp on her land, sometimes. From what I've heard, it's a run-down sort of show, and some of the men are little more than vagabonds. It could be that some of them decided to rob these two, and then killed them to stop the alarm being raised."

I sensed the tension in Holmes, as he struggled against the urge to laugh.

"A most interesting line of enquiry, sergeant. I wish you luck with it."

"Thank you. You gentlemen can go if you like. I left word at the station, so someone will come to help me with the bodies soon."

"Most commendable forethought," said Holmes. "Good day then, sergeant."

As I expected, a faint smile appeared on Holmes' lips as we left the scene.

"You deliberately misled him!" I protested when we were far enough away.

"To the contrary, I simply failed to disagree with his theory. Do you think he believes Cairns cut off his own hand, or did Blackthorne do it before he hit himself on the head? And where is the hand, now?"

"When he has taken the facts into consideration, his suppositions will collapse."

"By that time, we will have returned to Baker Street. After Lestrade has given us time before he intervenes, I cannot allow a country sergeant to get in the way, especially with the true nature of all this so nearly uncovered."

I thought my friend had adopted a most unreasonable attitude towards Grimes, and he seemed to sense this, for in a moment his expression had softened and he spoke in a different tone.

"Do not think me cruel, Watson, but to get bound up in a local police enquiry at this crucial stage in our investigation would ruin much that we have achieved. No doubt Sergeant Grimes is a good man, despite his limited powers of observation. That he has many fine qualities is evident, but like so many of the official force he lacks imagination. If that talent could be taken like medicine, a good dose would transform him into an officer at whose name the criminal classes would tremble."

"Holmes, how did the jester kill those men?" I asked when he lapsed into silence.

"First I will tell you how I know he was there, apart from the tracks. You will recall the broken-down stile that we crossed, before the discovery of the bodies?"

"You said he had gripped it, for support."

"Exactly. I pointed out where splinters had been torn from the wood because they were embedded in his hand."

"There was blood to suggest that."

"Quite. But neither of the corpses had a wounded hand; unless it was the amputated one that has disappeared, therefore the presence of a third person is undeniable. Now, I managed to ascertain the cause of both deaths, which were identical, while you were away. At first I saw nothing, but more detailed observation through my lens revealed a tiny spot of blood in one ear of each man."

"Such a wound is unlikely to be fatal."

"It is certain to be," he disagreed, "since it marks the entry of an extremely sharp instrument that has been driven into the brain. I would say that it was most likely a hypodermic needle, or a sharpened spoke from a bicycle wheel."

"My God, Holmes," I retorted, revolted by the deed, "who is this man who does such things?"

"Possibly the most remorseless criminal in England, or his accomplice. The fact that he was able to administer such a precise incision suggests that he stood close to his victims, without arousing their suspicions. He first struck Cairns with a club or other blunt instrument, and returned to him after dealing with Blackthorne."

"If only my bullet had killed him, those men would be alive still."

"Perhaps," he said indifferently, "but do not waste sympathy on those two. They both had a part in this business."

"Blackthorne is involved? Cairns' misdeeds are hardly surprising, when his reputation is considered, but I had not suspected the poacher."

"Blackthorne was rather more than a poacher. It is certain that his meeting with the jester was no chance encounter, though his fabricated account of it has earned him some momentary notoriety among his friends, and no doubt some free glasses of ale as well. No, it was he who helped to conceal the jester and supply him with food and drink." Holmes altered his stride to avoid a rabbit hole. "As for Cairns, you will recall my drawing your attention to the absence of brakes on his bicycle."

"I admit to some confusion regarding the significance."

"You will remember that I observed him to be in the habit of dragging his foot along the ground, to use his shoe as a substitute."

"Still, I can make nothing of it."

"Friction had worn his right shoe to an unusual shape. Consider now the tracks that we thought were made by a cripple, in the wood."

"As always, you make everything seem simple," I sighed. "Our task should be easier now at least, since we are looking for a wounded man."

"If I am right about the existence of an accomplice, he could remain hidden while the other takes his place."

"We could look for injury, among Lady Heminworth's familiars," I suggested.

"No doubt the opportunity to do so will present itself." He put a hand to his brow, to peer ahead. "But I see the turrets of Theobald Grange are within sight, and it is well past time for our luncheon."

The great studded door opened as Holmes raised his hand to knock, and the first sight of Walters' face told of something amiss.

"What has happened?" I cried as I hurried past him in the wake of my friend.

"It is Lady Heminworth, sir." His voice trembled. "She is beside herself with fear."

Still in our outer clothing, we entered the great hall to find her huddled in an armchair near the fireplace. A low wail escaped her as she stared at us with eyes that seemed not to see, and she showed no awareness of Miss Monkton, whose efforts to bring comfort were fruitless.

"When did this begin?" I asked quickly.

"I found her like this," Miss Monkton said as tears ran down her face, "no more than a few minutes ago. She sat shivering, with that look in her eyes, and would not answer me. Then Walters came because he had seen you from one of the windows."

I knelt before my patient, and felt a touch of despair as I looked into her dull eyes. I spoke to her in a gentle tone, but there was no sign that she heard me, and her skin had the pale sheen of the newly dead, though she still lived. She began to murmur excitedly, though we could understand none of her words. Then she was silent once more. I half-turned to speak to the others, when she spoke suddenly in a strange voice: "It is in the bedroom."

I turned to Holmes but he had already gone. Her Ladyship was left in the care of Miss Monkton as I followed hastily. My friend stood in a thoughtful posture at the foot of the bed.

"Cairns' missing hand is a mystery no more," he said.

I saw at once that the dead fingers had been bound with wire to curl the hand into a fist. Blood was all around it, spread like the petals of a flower across the pillow on Lady Heminworth's bed.

"Her Ladyship's relapse is also explained." I muttered coldly.

"Indeed." His eyes swept the panelled walls. "He could have entered anywhere. This house probably has a maze of concealed passages."

Holmes spent some minutes examining the hand before summoning Walters, then dispatching him to bring a canvas bag to contain it.

"I will take this to the edge of the wood and bury it," he told me, "while this room is cleaned and made presentable. Return to your patient, doctor, and I will join you shortly."

By the time my friend returned I had administered a stronger dose of laudanum and Lady Heminworth's confused speech drifted into peaceful lethargy. We stood with Miss Monkton near the doorway for, despite her Ladyship's stupor, it was as well to speak out of her hearing.

"This I have feared from the beginning," I whispered. "The shock of this latest outrage was too much."

"Has she, then, lost her sanity?" Miss Monkton's voice was taut with anxiety.

I considered this. "You must understand that my medical training was for the healing of physical ailments, not for those conditions which attack the mind," I began. "Nevertheless, experience and some research have enabled me to recognise certain symptoms when sanity has given way to madness. While I believe that your aunt's condition remains unstable, I think it unlikely that she has yet crossed the threshold into insanity. She must be put to bed without delay, and I will administer her medicine every few hours. It is imperative that she is kept warm and calm at all times, and she must not sleep alone tonight. Perhaps it could be arranged for one of the maids to sleep in her Ladyship's bedroom, within call?"

"That is unnecessary, I will do it."

"Better, still. She must retire now, but you need not remain with her yet. She will sleep deeply for a few hours."

Miss Monkton put an arm around her aunt's shoulders and helped her to rise and to ascend the first steps of the staircase, then she turned to face us, and I saw again the fierce spirit that her anger brought out.

"Gentlemen," she said with her eyes blazing, "this cannot continue. Redouble your efforts, I beg of you, to rid us of this scourge. I will do anything you ask of me, even to endangering my own life, to hasten the end of this threat by a moment." Tears glistened on her cheeks, then she looked past us and her expression changed. I saw that Walters stood silently awaiting instructions, which she gave in a voice that had at once lost its urgency.

"Please arrange for the cleaning of her Ladyship's room. Tonight we will both sleep in mine. Luncheon is already late, so we will take it immediately on my return."

Walters collected our coats and hats as the two women reached the top of the staircase and passed out of our sight along the gallery.

"That is a woman of fine spirit," Holmes observed, as if he had read my thoughts.

"I will allow time for Miss Monkton to prepare her Ladyship for her bed," I told him, "then I must attend her briefly to ensure that she sleeps peacefully."

I left him shortly after, and took my bag to Miss Monkton's room. When she admitted me, I saw that my patient slept.

"Her Ladyship did not resist?" I asked.

"Not at all."

"Nor try to communicate with you?"

"No. She was exhausted as we climbed the stairs, and fell deeply asleep once in bed."

"Excellent. The longer she sleeps, the more her strength is renewed." I put a hand on her shoulder. "Be brave, I will know more about her condition by tomorrow. As to its cause, Sherlock Holmes is far from beaten yet."

"But what if she is no better? Please, Doctor Watson, I could not bear to see my aunt taken to an asylum. I have heard terrible stories about those places."

"Put your mind at rest," I said reassuringly, "for such a course would be considered only if she were a danger to herself and others, and probably not even then. I am far from convinced that those places are beneficial, in any case. Now, if you will be so kind as to ask a maid to fetch a glass, I will mix a further draught. You must see that her Ladyship drinks this, should she awaken during the coming night."

During our late luncheon little was said, except for reassurances from both Holmes and myself, to keep up Miss Monkton's spirits. Immediately after the meal was finished she took a book to her room, so that she might be there should her aunt awake unexpectedly.

Holmes, appearing deep in some new train of thought, locked himself in his room after assuring me that we would meet before dinner. Feeling somewhat abandoned, I took refuge once more in the library, where I sought out a volume with a few chapters on emotional illnesses that resembled Lady Heminworth's condition.

I confess to falling asleep over my studies, to awaken shortly before dinner. In my room, I had dressed and pronounced my reflection satisfactory, when a small noise outside alerted me. I turned from the mirror and opened my door a crack to see into the corridor. Holmes stood gazing through a window at Maybell Wood, now a dark shadow in the dusk. He turned towards me and I saw at once that his expression was grave, and knew he blamed himself for her Ladyship's latest ordeal.

"This must serve as a lesson to us, Watson," he said, "not to underestimate the cunning of our enemy. The evening before last he might have killed you, and today he is the cause of Lady Heminworth's renewed distress. Before this I almost had him in my grasp, but now I must question some of my conclusions and so I cannot act. Miss Monkton was right, our efforts must be redoubled before this jester ruins a good and decent woman with as little concern as you or I would swat a fly."

I shook my head. "We still do not know why. What is his purpose?"

"We do know, now."

"What, then?"

"He wants the Eye of Africa."

"I have never heard of it. It sounds like the name of a ship."

By now we were descending the staircase, and would soon be within earshot of anyone in the room below. Holmes held a finger to his lips and we said no more.

Miss Monkton stood waiting for us, looking very ill at ease.

"How is your aunt, now?" I asked her.

Her eyes were dark with worry. "She sleeps soundly."

"That is good, for now."

"All the doors and windows are secured, I trust?" Holmes asked her.

"I gave instructions to Walters, earlier."

"And the wine cellar and the chapel door below?"

"The broken locks have been replaced by tradesmen from the village, and the outer door reinforced."

"Excellent. Now, here is our dinner. Difficult as it may be, we must try to keep to a normal routine as far as possible, if only to demonstrate to our adversary that his efforts to bring chaos upon this house have been unsuccessful."

It was indeed a fine meal. Holmes, usually an indifferent eater, probably appreciated the smoked salmon more than Miss Monkton or myself. Despite everything, he was at his most charming, and his good humour helped to raise us from our saddened state.

When dessert was over, we adjourned to the armchairs near the fire. Miss Monkton made an effort to be cheerful, striking up a light conversation while Holmes and I sipped our brandy. At length, he produced his pipe and began to fill it with the black shag that was his preference.

"You do not, I hope, object to the aroma of strong tobacco?" He asked her.

She smiled faintly. "No, indeed, I am quite used to it. My late uncle was rarely seen without his pipe."

Holmes inclined his head in acknowledgement, drawing the fragrant smoke deep into his lungs. His expression told me that his thoughts were likely occupied with a review of our recent adventures, perhaps searching for any helpful fact that had been overlooked.

"As well as you can remember, what kind of man is Donald Heminworth?" He asked suddenly.

Miss Monkton looked surprised, as I was, at the question.

"My infrequent meetings with him left me with the impression of a forthright and honourable man," she said. "I remember him for his love of adventure, sense of duty and willingness to make light of the errors of others." A look of disbelief crossed her face. "Mr Holmes, you cannot believe my cousin to be in any way responsible for our troubles."

"You could say with certainty then," he resumed after a puff at his pipe, "that were he aware of these events, he would return to England to defend and protect his mother?"

"I have no doubt of it."

"That is as I expected. But I see that both you and Dr Watson are weary, since you are both straining against the inclination to yawn. After such a trying day we will all be the better for a good night's rest, or at least as much of one as we are able to manage. Good night, Miss Monkton, we shall see what the morning brings."

"Call me at once if I am needed," I reminded her, rising as Holmes had done.

She ascended the staircase, and her footfalls echoed along the corridor before her door closed. We wished Walters good night as he began clearing away the dinner things, and he extinguished the lights when he heard us on the floor above.

"Why did you ask Miss Monkton about her cousin?" I asked Holmes as we neared our rooms. "You cannot suspect that he is behind this affair. No man would commit such acts against his own family."

His face half in shadow beside the glow of the single lamp he held to light our way, he replied. "No, though I remain convinced that he is the key to all that has happened. As to what family members will do against each other your convictions are, I am bound to say, drawn from your somewhat exaggerated faith in humanity." The flame flickered, and he moved the lamp further away. "I do not believe I ever related to you the case of Ishmael Trimmer, who succeeded in having his father declared insane after administering to him several doses of an obscure but highly potent drug. The unfortunate old gentleman was set to end his days in an asylum when I was called in by a relative, but he recovered to live nine more years in good health."

"What became of his son?" I asked, visualising the story this would make for one of the magazines I contribute to occasionally.

"Oh, his father had no compunction about sending him to prison, so he was deprived of his inheritance and his gambling debts went unpaid. When he was again a free man, if I remember correctly, his creditors had him beaten and he died from his injuries."

"A touching family story indeed," I said sarcastically. "A case you solved before we met, no doubt?"

"While living in Montague Street, I believe it was. If you need any further examples of how greed or passion can so easily transcend family affections, consider the case of Gustav Hohner, a Swedish glass-blower who settled in London with his wife and children. To be free, he butchered them in a cellar, making it appear to be the work of a neighbour, and all for the love of a woman who, outside his imagination, he hardly knew."

"Another past triumph?"

"I played a modest part in ensuring that justice was done, but the newspapers of the time, with my approval, made much of Scotland Yard's involvement."

"As ever." I smiled in the darkness. "Good night, Holmes."

He turned with his hand on the door-handle.

"Good night, Watson. Be prepared for an eventful day, for tomorrow we begin to bring this affair to its end. Sleep well."

Chapter Eight - The Stranger in the Wood

The next morning again proved to be overcast. I gazed at the grey sky from my bedroom window, determined that my mood would be unaffected by such a depressing sight.

Nothing could be heard from Holmes' room. I listened intently for his movements, but apart from the birds in Maybell Wood and the faint clatter of crockery from within the house, there was silence.

Hastily, I readied myself. Miraculously my face escaped the razor unscathed, and I left my room for Miss Monkton's chamber while still buttoning my morning coat. I saw no one in the corridor, and outside her door I paused to listen in the hope that her Ladyship still slept.

In a moment I heard the soft murmur of Miss Monkton's voice, and my knock was quickly answered. Her Ladyship lay in one of the four-poster beds with the sheets pulled up to her throat. I could see no change; her peculiar detachment seemed unaltered. She had the look of one who humours a child, a condescending expression that I found disturbing.

Yet Miss Monkton alarmed me more. Her face was drawn and haggard, with dark smudges around the eyes so that they appeared to have sunken into her skull. Her pallor told me at once that she had indeed slept little, and her black hair was in disarray.

"How is her Ladyship?" I asked.

"There has been hardly a sound or a movement from her."

"You have watched over her all through the night?"

She nodded wearily. "I could not risk her waking and thinking herself alone."

"Very well, but now the maids shall take turns."

"I cannot sleep." she protested. "Last night when I pledged my aid to you, I spoke sincerely."

"Of that I am certain," I said gently, "but you will be of little use in an exhausted state. I must insist that you retire now, or as soon as you have eaten."

She nodded her reluctant agreement and then, as weariness began to overwhelm her, she withdrew without another word.

I approached the bed and placed my hand on Lady Heminworth's forehead. Of high temperature there was no sign, but the absence of awareness in her eyes still caused me concern. Her true self was imprisoned in a remote place.

"Lady Heminworth," I whispered, "can you hear me?"

She gave no sign that she could. I passed my hand quickly before her eyes and she did not flinch, nor did her benign stare alter. I took one of her hands in mine and pressed gently. There was no answering pressure. I pressed again, and a tiny movement of her fingers told me of her efforts to respond. As I lowered the limp arm to the blanket I realized that Miss Monkton had returned.

"There has been little improvement," I told her, "but I cannot see that her condition will worsen. As I suspected, this is not madness, it is the result of a severe shock. The effects on a sensitive personality are little known, and so I can do no more than see that she is kept comfortable."

"Is there nothing anyone can do?" she asked sadly.

Helpless, but desperate to aid both women, I searched my memory.

"While serving in India," I recalled, "I had a colleague whose interests lay in curing illnesses of the mind. He had some success treating young soldiers who had yet to be battle-hardened, men who became rigid with fear following their first encounters with the enemy. He came to recognise that this condition does not spring from cowardice, but from susceptibility to shock. After

135

leaving the army he established a practice in Brighton, in a large house away from the town where I once visited him. He treats troubled patients such as your aunt, and keeps a small trained and dedicated staff. I correspond with him occasionally and he reports some extraordinary triumphs."

"But what is the treatment?"

I chose my words carefully, so she should not think I described a charlatan. "It is not such as you might expect. He has no use for bars or whips or treadmills, but seeks to relax the mind so that the effects of shock are reversed. His tools are peace, the sea air and the absence of responsibility and fear, together with the patience and the understanding of the doctors and nurses. I came to respect his methods."

She glanced at her aunt, then back at me. "Can this be the answer, without the cruel methods I have heard about? Dr Watson, who is this man?"

"You will not have heard of him, for he is little known outside his profession. His name is Dr Phineas Turville."

As I expected, this meant nothing to her. "And you believe he could help?"

"I think there is a good chance of it." I heard movement in the great hall below. "But for now, I suggest that you summon a maid to watch over her Ladyship before we join Mr. Holmes at breakfast."

I ensured that my patient was comfortable before leaving the room. Downstairs, Holmes was already seated at the table, and I sensed at once the air of a hunting dog about him, straining at the leash. He listened attentively as I related all that had passed between Miss Monkton and myself.

"You have confidence in this man, I suppose?" he asked after enquiring about Lady Heminworth's condition. "When medical practitioners explore new territory, there are always some whose imaginative dreams far outweigh their powers."

"I have witnessed the results of his treatment, on several patients," I retorted rather indignantly. "Surely you, Holmes, who often employ unconventional methods yourself, know that a new direction can sometimes be a vast step forward."

He smiled at my outburst. "Then, on your recommendation, let us summon Dr. Turville, and hope that he will come. As soon as breakfast is finished, I will take the brougham into Armington Magna to despatch a telegram to him, if you will be so good as to write down anything of a technical nature that you wish him to know in advance. I have to visit the village, in any case."

"But you have already left the house this morning."

He inclined his head towards me, and raised an eyebrow. "And how, Watson, did you deduce that?"

"When I awake in an adjacent room to you, and can neither hear movement nor smell tobacco, and then encounter you with traces of mud on your boots, it seems fairly obvious."

"Bravo, Watson!" He laughed. "You are learning my methods well."

"Shall I accompany you then, to the village?"

Holmes considered. "No, I would be easier in my mind if you remained here."

"But there is no danger until after dusk, you said so yourself."

"I did indeed," he nodded in agreement, "but that was when the jester confined his activities to that time of the evening. Consider his exploits since then; your encounter in the cellar, the appearance of the disembodied hand, and so on, and you will see why I am concerned. It may be significant also that you saw him run away in the normal manner, rather than disappear, when the time and place of his escape were different. You will recall that I announced last night my intention to begin the end of this affair

137

today, and I have been out already as you observed, to further examine the exterior of the house and the edge of Maybell Wood."

My friend wore his most circumspect look, and I knew better than to ask about his progress. I have learned, during our long association, that Sherlock Holmes rarely confides his conclusions until he is satisfied that the puzzle is truly solved, and that his plans for counterattack are laid.

"We can expect to capture the jester soon then, this time?"

I had not intended it, but I saw that my reference to his previous unfounded optimism had exposed a sore point. Holmes had immense pride in his work, and I had no doubt that he held himself to blame for the continuing danger to Miss Monkton and her aunt.

"I have learned much about our adversary since then," he replied after a moment's thought. "It is true that I had come to certain conclusions quite erroneously, mainly because I underestimated his cunning. We know now that he is a skilled and accomplished criminal who will stop at nothing to attain his goals, but my hand is almost upon him and he is nearer to meeting the hangman than he realises."

"Then I will remain here, close to the women with my revolver within reach until your return from the village, if you wish it."

"Capital! It would be a sad day were my Watson no longer beside me."

As always when Holmes uttered such accolades, recollections of our comradeship during many adventures came to mind. My reminiscences were cut short quickly, since Miss Monkton descended the stairs and joined us.

"My aunt awoke briefly," she told us. "I explained about our intention to consult Dr Turville, but of course she could not understand."

"It may be that she understands, but cannot show it," I speculated. "I am not sufficiently familiar with her condition to be certain. Doubtlessly, Dr Turville will be able to tell us."

"I shall call at the post office immediately after breakfast," Holmes told Miss Monkton before she could speak. "No time must be lost in beginning her Ladyship's treatment."

"But not here," I said emphatically. "Lady Heminworth must leave this house. I remember your reasons that she should remain here, Holmes, but I now consider it essential that she is removed to another place. It is certain that Dr Turville will agree."

There was a short silence while breakfast was served. Holmes ate indifferently, as he always did when a problem confronted him.

"I have a suggestion to offer," Miss Monkton said as she laid down her knife and fork.

"Pray do so," my friend replied.

She hesitated until Walters had poured coffee and withdrawn. "As I see our difficulty, it would be best if my aunt were taken elsewhere for treatment, yet to remove her would discourage our enemy from acting further until her return."

"Precisely," agreed Holmes. "In addition, I fear that he may have the means to follow her, and then we would be powerless to help."

"I understand," she nodded, "but what if she left with our adversary believing that she remained at the house?"

"How could that be accomplished?" I asked.

Holmes smiled at her approvingly. "I believe that I have already considered the course you are about to propose. To exchange places with her Ladyship is a deception that you could maintain for a short while, of that I have no doubt. The difficulties that such a situation presents are not insurmountable, yet I must reject this as a strategy. The danger to your person would be such that I cannot, in good conscience, countenance it."

I saw again the fiery gleam in Miss Monkton's eyes, and knew that she would not be put off.

"And yet, Mr Holmes," she said with a hint of outrage, "you have allowed my aunt, who is less able than I, to continue living in the midst of this very same danger."

He did not reply immediately, appearing to take refuge in his thoughts rather than begin a heated discussion. Finally he raised his head to look at her with an expression that had she but known it, was his ultimate compliment to her bravery.

"Very well, it shall be as you say," he told her quietly, "but Dr Watson or I must be with you at all times, I will hear no argument on that. At night we will stand watch outside your door, alternating every three or four hours, and the bell-pull must always be within your reach."

She looked relieved. "I swear to do as you instruct."

"Excellent." He abandoned the remains of his coffee and got to his feet. "Now I would be obliged if you would arrange for the brougham to be brought to the front of the house. There are some errands I must attend to, as well as communicating with Dr. Turville, so it is better if I drive myself. Watson, if you would be so good as to write down anything that you wish me to tell him, as we discussed, that would be helpful."

I scribbled a few lines in my notebook while Walters received his instructions. Holmes put on his hat and coat and waited with suppressed impatience until he heard the clatter of hooves outside. He had no need to remind me of my duties, as he had done on his departure to London, and I believe he saw this in my face, for he merely smiled and nodded before striding to the door with a word of farewell.

With Miss Monkton, I watched from the doorway as the eager horse trotted around the edge of the lawn before turning into the long drive. As I made to follow her back into the house, distant movement caught my eye. I stopped and stared and saw that Rawlings, wearing a tweed cap that I had seen before, also watched Holmes' departure.

The remainder of the morning passed without incident. Conversation with Miss Monkton was difficult, because concern for her aunt occupied her mind. Presently I went to my room to read, leaving my door open so that I would be alerted by the slightest note of alarm in the hushed voices of Miss Monkton or the maid, who were now with her Ladyship. In this way those few hours passed, and my hand was never far from my revolver. At last I took out my pocket-watch, to find that lunch would shortly be served, and it was then that I heard the brougham returning.

At lunch, Holmes confirmed that the telegram to Dr. Turville had been despatched, and I saw hope in Miss Monkton's face. Walters served a thick vegetable soup, but before any of us could eat we heard a foot upon the stairs. As one, we three turned to see her Ladyship descending, with the maid steadying her steps.

"I'm sorry, Miss," the maid said to Miss Monkton. "I could do nothing to stop her."

"She spoke to you, then?"

"No, Miss, her Ladyship rose from her bed as if she were sleepwalking. It was all I could do to guide her on the stairs."

The maid was dismissed and I assisted Miss Monkton in settling her aunt at the table. Holmes' expression was grave, as he greeted her Ladyship without response.

"This is not unusual in such cases," I told him when I had ascertained that her Ladyship was oblivious to our presence. "Despite her state of shock, her body seeks nourishment."

"I understand," was his only reply. His eyes were on Miss Monkton, who seemed to possess an inner strength that refused to allow her to give way to tears. Lady Heminworth wore her empty smile like a mask and presently ate a little food. I noted that her movements had an unnatural quality, like those of someone in a trance-like state. Shortly after the meal she returned to her room aided by her maid, having spoken not a word, and I followed to administer her medicine.

A short while later Miss Monkton re-joined her aunt, leaving Holmes and I alone. Soon torrential rain began to fall, beating heavily upon the windowpanes. The afternoon had turned bleak.

We drank two cups of strong Assam tea before Walters appeared, to clear away and enquire as to our further needs. A loud pounding on the door began, making more noise than the rain, whereupon he excused himself to cross the great hall and withdraw the latch.

The door opened to admit a sodden figure, a phantom-like form that stumbled into the room. Holmes and I peered into the half-light, to see the face of Rawlings revealed when the thick hood of his old oilskin was hastily pushed back. He ignored the hand that Walters offered to relieve him of his drenched coat and strode towards us, leaving a wet trail across the stone floor.

"Mr Holmes!" he cried. "I have news!"

His appearance was alarming, for his long hair had been plastered flat by the windblown rain and he was in a state of great excitement.

Holmes had already risen to his feet. "Rawlings! What is it? Are you injured?"

"No, sir. Begging your pardon for the interruption, but I have seen him in the woods. I came to tell you as quickly as I could."

I saw Holmes' body grow tense. "Who have you seen?"

But Rawlings was prevented from answering by a fit of coughing, and he controlled his breathing with difficulty. Holmes brought a glass of brandy from the decanter.

"A stranger," he gasped when he had sipped the harsh liquid and his chest began to subside, "a tall man with an evil look who ran when I called to him. Such a man as you asked me to watch for, Mr Holmes, I do not think he has any business on the estate."

I recalled Holmes telling me of his belief that our enemy no longer intended to confine himself to appearances at dusk.

"When was this?" I asked Rawlings.

"Not fifteen minutes ago, Doctor. The rain forced me to take shelter under the great oak near Grover's cottage."

"You were out, in this weather?"

He nodded, swallowing the last of his brandy. "One of the horses was frightened by the noise of the storm."

Holmes had put on his hat and coat. "Thank you, Rawlings. I see that the rain has lessened somewhat, so you should have no difficulty returning to your quarters. No, it is not necessary to accompany me, I know the place you speak of, although I doubt our intruder will be there now. Still, it will serve as a starting point."

Walters showed Rawlings to the door and I went to my friend.

"Holmes, are you armed?"

"No. An oversight on my part, perhaps."

"Then take my revolver." I reached into my pocket.

He hesitated. "Thank you, old fellow, but your need may be greater."

"You will need to hurry, the ground must be sodden."

"That will not affect my progress too much, I think. You will recall that Rawlings told us he saw this man near Grover's cottage, no more than fifteen minutes before he stood here relating the incident to us. I believe I can get there in less time than that."

"I will come with you."

"You forget you are the women's protector. As before, remain close to them and on no account allow yourself to be separated from your pistol. Expect attack from any quarter."

He turned abruptly towards the door and was gone. I watched from the window, but the rain beat down with renewed ferocity that soon hid him from sight. For an hour I sat in an armchair, smoking and listening for any summons from the ladies.

I became drowsy, but the reappearance of Walters shocked me back to wakefulness. In his stiff manner, he walked across the room to answer the door. For an instant I wondered that I had not heard the caller's knock, until I realised that the brass bell-pull outside must be connected to the butler's pantry.

The door closed, and Walters approached me holding a tray on which he had placed a yellow envelope.

"A telegram has just arrived for you, sir," he said, and I thanked him and took out the folded sheet the moment he left.

A wave of relief swept over me. It was from Turville! He was to arrive at Armington Magna on the morning train. I fidgeted in my chair, impatient to tell my friend or Miss Monkton of this wonderful news.

I hardly had time to consider the effects of this welcome new development, when Walters appeared once more. This time I followed him to the door because I expected Holmes at any minute. I saw that it was he, and waited as Walters took his soaked outer clothing.

"Holmes, I have good news!" I cried when the butler had left us.

"Ha! Dr Turville has undoubtedly agreed to visit us."

"How did you know?" I asked, feeling somewhat deflated.

"I saw the telegram boy ride away from the house. The poor fellow was drenched and could hardly ride his bicycle against the strong wind."

"Let us hope he escapes pneumonia. Turville arrives tomorrow."

"Capital!" Holmes poured himself a small brandy and rubbed his hands. "Perhaps the weather will have improved by then. It is bleak out there."

"Did you find the stranger?" I asked him after he had sipped his drink and lapsed into thought, with no apparent intention of referring to the incident.

"Oh yes," he replied absently. "He was not our man, but that was not unexpected."

It seemed he would say no more, but my impatience would not be contained. "Holmes, will you not tell me about it?"

His expression altered as he emerged from his contemplation. "My dear Watson, you must forgive my bad manners. I was speculating on how this affair will end, as it soon must. No matter, I will tell you everything that transpired, from the moment I left this house."

"Please, I am all anticipation."

My friend leaned back in his chair. "First, using the concealment of the storm, I watched for the first ten minutes or so to ensure that this house was not under observation."

"You suspected a trick to lure you away while our enemy gained entry?"

"Precisely. When I was satisfied, I made my way to Grover's cottage and took up a similar post. After watching the windows carefully I saw no movement, but in order to be certain I knocked loudly at the door. As there was no response I tried the latch and to my surprise I found that Mr Grover is in the habit of leaving his door unlocked. No doubt he feels safe in doing this in the middle of the wood."

"Rather foolish I would have thought, with the jester and now this stranger wandering about."

"Patience, Watson." Holmes smiled. "I entered the cottage to clear up a small mystery left unsolved since our previous visit. You will recall that Grover attempted to conceal something before admitting us. Now, standing there, it was clear that there was no hiding place except for under the bed."

"And what did you find there?"

"Nothing that connects him to this affair. This man deserves our sympathy, not our condemnation. A small case, hidden beneath the bed-frame, contained two miniature portraits and several documents. The likenesses were of his wife and daughter, whom he was convicted of murdering, and one of the papers was a pardon for his supposed crimes. The real murderer confessed on his deathbed years later, and Grover was released from prison. To this day he is a broken man, and so his attitude to others and his preference for solitude are easily understood."

"Indeed," I said. "I imagine there was some doubt about his sanity, as he escaped the rope?"

Holmes nodded. "The other documents revealed as much, but his derangement was probably the result of severe grief. The kindest thing would be to leave him alone with whatever memories he has left, since he plays no part in our investigation."

"A tragic story. What of the man Rawlings saw?"

"I left the cottage and followed the path to Armington Magna, keeping just within the trees that border on it. Grover was taking a leisurely walk with the man whom Rawlings described to us, although I could see nothing evil about him. I confronted the pair immediately, rather surprising them, and asked the gamekeeper to explain his companion's presence. By this time I had concluded that it was unlikely that either of these men meant harm to anyone, but I was unprepared when the stranger bowed his head and beseeched me not to call the police. Grover explained that this was a man he had known in prison, a fellow inmate who had contracted an incurable disease there. The man's poor physical condition suggested that he has not long to live, and I felt bound to send him on his way with a half-sovereign in his pocket."

"A poor soul like that cannot be the jester."

"Quite. And so it seems that my first conclusions were correct, despite misleading evidence to the contrary."

In an instant, his meaning came to me. "Then, after all, Rawlings is behind this?"

Holmes nodded grimly. "Rawlings it was who planned everything that has happened here, with some assistance. Say nothing to anyone yet, for we still have to gain sufficient proof. As for now, I suggest that we repair to our rooms until dinner when, if Miss Monkton is rested, we will make our plans."

Just before ten o'clock the next morning I paced the single platform of Armington Magna station. The brougham I had left in the care of a porter, who had taken the opportunity to enjoy a quiet smoke in the lane.

Last night, I had seen Miss Monkton finally succumb to exhaustion. Her fitful sleep of the afternoon had done little to renew her strength, so that she was all but carried to her room by one of the maids who then remained with the two women through the night.

Before that, the three of us dined and Holmes outlined his proposal, omitting only his conclusion about Rawlings, and Miss Monkton agreed at once. Her uncharacteristic lack of questions and comments I attributed to her weariness that became more evident as we talked.

My thoughts were interrupted as a tall plume of smoke appeared some distance down the line. The group of locals waiting further along the platform drew back as the train roared into the station, losing speed and billowing steam and smoke. The iron wheels shrieked and threw up sparks, before the coaches came to rest and the first passengers began to appear.

I watched the parade of people giving up their tickets to an elderly station master. Two young children skipped across the platform until a sharp word from a parent or nanny brought them to an abrupt halt, and several severely dressed men carried document cases or rolled newspapers, giving each other aloof stares. It seemed no one else would emerge until a young couple appeared, accompanied by a chaperone who looked on with elderly disapproval. This procession had occupied my attention; so that I almost missed the heavily-built man wearing a top hat that made him look taller still, stepping down from the last coach of the train.

"Watson!" Two long strides and he stood before me, dropping his carpet-bag heedlessly. His hands gripped my shoulders and he smiled broadly. "How long has it been?" He stepped back to regard me at arm's length. "Never mind, you've hardly changed. You are perhaps a little stouter, but no more so than I."

"Never," I laughed. "You, Turville, are the same as ever."

He shook my hand with a firm grip. "I can't tell you, old fellow, how good it is to see you again. I never dreamed that you, of all people, would bring me a case."

He gave a great guffaw and I knew that this was the Turville I knew of old. Like Holmes, he was a tall man, but thick set and with a genial disposition that was suggested by the permanent creases around his eyes and corners of his mouth.

"But it has been an unhappy affair." I remarked sadly.

"And you believe that I can improve matters?"

"We are praying that you can."

He nodded, pleasantly. "Then we shall see what can be done."

He picked up his bag and I led him out of the station. We settled ourselves in the brougham and I tipped the porter before taking the reins. For the first few minutes Turville appeared to exult in the leafy lanes around us, closing his eyes and taking in deep breaths of the Warwickshire air. I had felt the same myself on first arriving, after the soot and grime of London which neither Holmes nor I had left for months.

"I have read much of your association and adventures with Mr Sherlock Holmes," Turville said above the clatter of hooves on the wet road. "It surprised me to receive a telegram from him. I see from his rather concise phrasing that I am required to attend a lady involved in one of your escapades. I must say, Watson, you have done me a service in calling on me. In some ways, Mr Holmes'

149

methods of observation are not so different from those of my own profession."

In his jovial way, he talked incessantly until we saw the distant roofs of Theobald Grange. I had spoken little, only contributing here and there a word that was invariably lost in his torrent of enthusiasm for his work and for life. I was glad that he did not pursue his enquiries regarding the situation at Theobald Grange or the nature of the case, for I wished Holmes to explain so that I could watch the effect of each man upon the other.

Thankfully, the rains of yesterday had not persisted. Now, as we entered the long drive, the sun burst through the clouds as though to approve Turville's arrival, like an omen foretelling that the dark shadow over Lady Heminworth would soon be lifted.

From the instant that the house came fully into view, Turville began a favourable commentary on its architectural aspects and appearance. The fearful gloom about the place which had so impressed me at first sight was apparently lost on him.

I reined in the horse near the steps, and the main door opened at once. Holmes and Miss Monkton appeared, and I made the introductions just as Rawlings approached to relieve me of the brougham. I was careful not to vary my manner, which might alert him to our knowledge of his crimes, but I read much into Holmes' stare at the man's retreating back.

Turville was received in a most warm and friendly manner, and in a short while we were seated around the fire in the great hall, each with a glass of excellent port.

"It would be as well if I am acquainted with the symptoms of her Ladyship's condition, before I see her," Turville said in his usual mild manner, "along with your perception of the source of her anxiety. Your observations, gentlemen, and of course yours, Miss Monkton, will allow me to discount some possible methods of treatment as inappropriate, and will doubtlessly set me on the true path."

Each of us in turn related our impressions of Lady Heminworth's recent history, and I remembered Turville's earlier remark. His methods did indeed bear a resemblance to those of Holmes, even his way of sitting with his hands pressed together as he listened, reminded me of the habits of my friend. When we had all spoken, Turville sat in silence, his brow furrowed in concentration.

"The onset of the illness, then," he said at last, "was brought about by her Ladyship's fear of an apparition that represents itself as supernatural. It's menace was reinforced by the loss of two members of her family, and the harmful effects are enhanced by her naturally sensitive and superstitious nature."

"We believe that her disposition is the reason for our enemy's chosen method of attack," Holmes remarked.

"He has perceived a weakness and is making use of his knowledge," Turville agreed. "What treatment have you prescribed, Watson?"

"Extract of laudanum, in measured doses, together with plenty of sleep."

He considered this. "Probably that was the best that could be done at the time. As I understand it, the purpose of these outrages is not known?"

I looked at once at Holmes, wondering how much of our suspicions to reveal, but his expression was impassive as he answered Turville.

"He appears to blame Lady Heminworth and her family for events that took place in Norman times. The costume he wears confirms this and suggests that he is himself deranged."

"Undoubtedly," Turville said. "In fact, I would welcome the chance to study him, before the hangman does his work. Are you near to capturing him, Mr Holmes?"

My friend made a non-committal gesture. "It has been a difficult case. Twice, when I had thought him to be in my grasp, he eluded me. Watson, also, came near to apprehending him."

"These gentlemen have taken on our cause at great risk to themselves," Miss Monkton told Turville. "But they are too modest. By now my aunt would surely have become a victim and possibly myself also, had it not been for their presence and protection."

"Doubtlessly, that is true. It is clear to me that she must be removed to another place without delay." Turville had made his decision, and I decided not to remind Holmes that this was my original conclusion also. "My clinic at Brighton will afford her Ladyship a complete change of surroundings. I consider this vital to her recovery since associations with this house have evidently intensified her fears. In addition, she will be physically distant from her tormentor."

I saw a hint of disapproval in Holmes' eyes, instantly gone as his compassion overcame his objection. We had agreed our plan of substitution, but I knew he would have preferred Lady Heminworth to remain here, were it not for the reasons that Turville put forward.

"One thing more, before I meet my patient," he said to Miss Monkton. "I must know how she appears to you, physically, compared to her usual self."

"My aunt's face is expressionless, like that of a mannequin," she said sadly. "She stares into the distance, and seems unaware of those near to her. No words can be enticed from her, except when she occasionally becomes lucid and then she speaks in riddles. Usually, she appears detached and to believe herself alone."

"Her thoughts are in turmoil." Turville got to his feet and began pacing in a circular path around the hearth. He took from his pocket a silver case that he offered to Holmes and myself. It contained little green cigars that proved to have rather aromatic properties, but were a little mild for my taste.

I noted that Holmes watched Turville with interest. It was certain that by now he had formed his opinion of the man, and decided how much of our intentions he should know. My friend would, I knew, have gleaned more from Turville's words and demeanour than any of us.

The hour for luncheon came, and by the intimate nature of the conversation between Holmes and Turville, I formed the impression that our visitor would indeed be taken into our confidence regarding the secret departure of Lady Heminworth.

"And so, Dr. Turville," said Holmes some little time after the remains of the meal had been cleared away, "are you able to give us any hope regarding Lady Heminworth? I appreciate of course, that you have not yet seen your patient, and it may therefore be premature to express an opinion, but I wondered if her symptoms have revealed anything of significance?"

Turville smiled. "They have indeed, Mr Holmes, and I have no doubt that I can assist her Ladyship on her journey towards recovery. However, I should point out that the healing of the mind can take much time. Also, the extent of success is always governed by the strength of the patient's will to recover. Complete co-operation is vital."

"I believe that the Austrian, Dr Sigmund Freud, has established this also in a treatment he describes as 'psychoanalysis'," I recalled.

"Quite so, although his methods are somewhat different from my own. There is, however, a common starting point, which is always the initial examination of the patient. Therefore, if her Ladyship is ready, I propose to delay no further. The best place would be her bedchamber, not only for privacy but because it represents to her a sanctuary, where she has so far come to no harm."

"She sleeps in my room since her illness returned, so that I am there if she needs me in the night." Miss Monkton did not mention that this had been since the discovery of the severed hand in her aunt's bedchamber, and I saw Holmes glance in her direction approvingly.

"Then that is where the examination shall be." Turville agreed, turning to her. "You will, of course, be present throughout, although I must request that you remain silent until the proceedings are concluded."

"May I be present also?" I asked him.

"My dear fellow, I had considered that settled," Turville beamed. "This is a very new science, and the observations of other doctors are most desirable, so that they can see for themselves both the method and the results. Only, I beg of you, Watson, try to contain yourself if the outcome should differ from your expectations, and maintain the essential silence that I have mentioned."

"You have my word," I assured him, "but expect a deluge of questions when you are finished."

He smiled his understanding and looked towards Sherlock Holmes, I thought to invite him to witness the proceedings with us.

"No, thank you, doctor," said my friend, as if he had read Turville's mind. "There is still much to consider about this case. I shall remain here until you arrive at your diagnosis."

"As you wish, Mr Holmes," said Turville with some surprise. "I will share with you such findings as may assist you."

On the stairs I looked back once to see that Holmes was already lost in thought.

Lady Heminworth sat fully dressed in an armchair beside the bed. The maid left the room, carrying a tray of food that was hardly touched. I thought her Ladyship looked slightly improved since I saw her last, but her vague smile was unaltered.

I think Miss Monkton would have introduced him, but Turville held up a hand. That he was familiar with the symptoms of the condition I saw at once, and felt a stab of apprehension as his face became grave.

"Please be so good as to half-draw the curtains," he said in a tone that was more serious than normal. "Miss Monkton, if you will be seated near the window, Watson can stand behind me where observation will be easier. Please remember the importance of silence."

When all was ready he spoke softly to his patient as he examined her eyes, looking closely at the whites as well as the pupils while her distant expression remained unaltered. After a while he stepped back to look into her face, speaking in a voice that was at the same time reassuring and strangely penetrative. This continued for some time until I felt that, had I not been sworn to silence, it would have been wise to advise him that his labours were fruitless. His voice had changed imperceptibly, taking on a tone that was almost hypnotic, to the extent that even I felt its relaxing effect.

Then I saw a flicker of awareness in Lady Heminworth's eyes. Turville held up a finger and passed it horizontally, inches from her face. Surprise replaced her frozen expression, and her eyes followed his movement. The drone of his voice had become almost an incantation, and now her head turned after his hand.

Smiling into her eyes, he brought his finger to his lips so that her gaze rested there, watching them form quiet words. He took one of her hands and pressed it gently as I had done earlier, but attracting a far greater response. Again, the thought came to me that her body had become the prison of her mind, and if that were so then Turville had discovered the key. Miss Monkton drew in a sharp breath, as hope lit up her face.

"I shall leave you now, and you must rest," Turville whispered to her Ladyship. "Soon I will take you to a place where there is no fear or worry, where nothing can harm you. There you will complete the journey that you have begun, you will come back to us fully restored to your former self. You will again be happy and without any fear, because that which troubled you has been taken away, and cannot return." He paused, watching her closely. "It will never return."

I saw that her eyes had become heavy with sleep, and she had the air of one who has relinquished a heavy burden. That her tension had eased was reflected in the softening of her expression. I wondered if Turville had mesmerised her.

He gestured to Miss Monkton and myself, and we left the room before him. I had begun to wonder what Holmes would make of this miracle when Turville joined us in the corridor, closing the door softly behind him.

"She sleeps," he said. "I think for several hours, at least."

"Will she recover?" Miss Monkton asked anxiously. "Please tell me that this nightmare has come to an end."

Turville put a finger to his lips to indicate the need for silence, and we moved away from the bedchamber.

"I cannot guarantee any success, as long as she remains here," he whispered, "but I feel that she has an excellent chance if you will entrust her to me."

"We must discuss this with Holmes," I told him before Miss Monkton could speak. "He has foreseen this situation."

My friend sat in contemplation as I had last seen him, the surrounding air heavy with the aroma of his tobacco.

"I have just witnessed a remarkable consultation, Holmes," I said in answer to his expectant look. "Turville was able to draw a response from Lady Heminworth."

"Capital!" he retorted. "Does this suggest, then, that she will recover?"

"If she is removed from these surroundings and receives treatment, that is more likely," Turville advised.

"That is essential?"

156

"I consider it so."

Holmes nodded. "You intend taking her to your clinic, then?"

"It would be best."

"If it must be, we should make arrangements quickly. Watson and I will attempt to resolve things so that all will be well for her return. How is her Ladyship, now?"

"She is asleep," Miss Monkton said. "Dr Turville's examination proved exhausting for her. Lily has resumed her watch until I take her place later."

"Excellent. Dr Turville, I take it that you are in agreement with Watson that any further strain would likely cause irreversible damage to her Ladyship's health?"

"It would probably cause her to retreat into herself, so far as to be unreachable by anyone. Such conditions are sometimes permanent."

"Then you will doubtless also agree that to apprehend the tormentor responsible is the sure way to prevent this?"

Turville looked at Holmes curiously, uncertain as to his purpose in stating the obvious. "Indeed, I know you will spare nothing on her behalf, while I attempt to bring her Ladyship to her former self. She will be quite safe, in Brighton."

"How I wish I could concur. As it is, our adversary has proved to be both merciless and resourceful. We have reason to suppose that he knows much that goes on in this house, and so I consider it probable that he will follow her to continue his reign of terror."

"That would be disastrous, Mr Holmes, but if you foresee it then I must take it into account, for I am faced also with the difficulty of admitting Lady Heminworth to my clinic without endangering the other patients. The obvious solution, that of solitary incarceration, would be contrary to the treatment I propose."

"Quite." Holmes leaned forward in his chair, and I saw that he was about to confide in Turville. "It seems we find ourselves with a dilemma. The answer, surely, is for you to remove your patient while our enemy is encouraged to believe that she has remained here."

Turville's usually cheerful expression became grim. "Can that be brought about? As his identity is unknown to you, and his ways of obtaining information are not clear, it is a terrible risk." He stopped. "Mr Holmes, is it known why he does these things?"

"The picture is as yet incomplete," Holmes replied evasively, "but my suspicions are becoming more firmly rooted every day. However, our enemy must be forced to reveal himself, so that proof may be given to the authorities. To this end, Miss Monkton, at her own suggestion, has a vital part to play, as do you, if you will assist us."

Turville's usual mild expression returned to his face. "Towards restoring Lady Herminworth's health, I will gladly do anything within my power. If you have devised a way for her to leave this house undetected then let us put it to the test, so that her treatment can begin that much sooner. You have only to explain what is required of me."

"Good man!" I exclaimed, realising that I should have known better than to have had any doubt. For an instant I felt that all our fears had receded, then I chanced to glance through the window at the darkening sky as Walters appeared to light the lamps. The early evening held the last of the setting sun and a figure passed across the glass, afire with golden rays.

I believe that Holmes had already noticed my alarm, for his head turned at once to the window. We rose together as a dreadful scream pierced the silence.

Chapter Ten - Death of an Unknown Woman

"Great heavens!" exclaimed Turville. "What was that?"

"I think you are about to see the jester for yourself, doctor," Holmes told him. "Miss Monkton, pray go to your aunt and see that the curtains are closely drawn and her window closed. There must be no risk of her seeing this spectacle again."

She left immediately, her footsteps fast on the stairs as we gathered around the window. Walters stood as if frozen, a burning taper in his hand, until a murmured word from Holmes sent him from the room.

"You see before you the instigator of this family's troubles," Holmes told Turville, "and possibly the murderer of Lady Heminworth's husband and elder son."

The hideous mask caught a glint of the dying light. The jester danced and somersaulted before bowing as an actor does on concluding his performance. I heard Turville gasp at the vehemence of the shouted obscenities and threats of death that followed. This surprised me as I had imagined he would be familiar with such outbursts in the course of his profession. A short prayer escaped his lips, and I fancied he was beseeching the Almighty to make his skills equal to the task ahead.

"Great God in heaven!" he cried in astonishment. "It is now no mystery to me why that poor woman is reduced to such a state. He sounds like a demon from Hell!"

"How hard he strives to give that impression." said Holmes. "Her Ladyship's superstitious nature makes it believable to her, but we are unafraid of a madman wearing a mask."

"His ravings are directed against her," I observed, "yet she is not present."

"He cannot see us clearly. The window reflects the sunset."

"I have my revolver here. This should end, now."

My friend held up a hand before I could move. "No, Watson, I would not like to see the hangman cheated, and there are more involved than this. Also, our first concern must be to quickly remove him from Lady Heminworth's sight. However, if you must have your sport, fire to scare him away."

The jester ceased his pirouetting and ran into the falling darkness as Holmes opened the window casement. It seemed to me that he had expected us to come to the door, allowing him time to get to the wood. I fired twice into the gloom, with such poor aim as to make any wounding accidental. He faded into the trees, clearly unhurt. A final screeched threat was lost on the night air.

"Thank God her Ladyship did not witness that," Turville said when we were again seated. "Mr Holmes, you implied, I think, that there are others concerned in this affair?"

"Indeed. That is why we mounted no pursuit. I want none of the fish to escape the net."

Turville nodded, and I began to question him about his diagnosis and forthcoming treatment of Lady Heminworth. I saw from Holmes' expression that he knew my intentions, for my enquiries were as much to divert Turville's attention from our experience as for my own information.

Miss Monkton returned to us for dinner, with the news that her aunt had slept peacefully throughout the incident. On hearing our account of the exchange, she immediately questioned the wisdom of allowing the jester's escape, and again Holmes stated his intentions.

"Is his capture really so near, Mr Holmes?" She asked uncertainly.

"You may depend upon it."

"And are your plans complete?"

"They are."

"Is there any reason then, why we cannot discuss them?"

"None. If you would be good enough to excuse me, for a moment."

My friend rose and left the table. We watched as he took four of the unoccupied dining chairs to the centre of the Great Hall, beneath the chandelier, and arranged them in a circle. After a short interval, during which he put his ear to the panelling and rapped upon it several times along each wall, he beckoned to us to join him.

When we were all again seated, Turville looked around him incredulously. "Are we to hold a séance, Mr Holmes?"

"Not at all. I thought it as well to take what precautions we can, since our enemy is sometimes able to learn our intentions."

Miss Monkton also wore a slightly puzzled expression and so, knowing something of Holmes' ways, I explained.

"Our chairs are placed together in the exact centre of the room because it is the furthest point from all four walls, where hidden passages might exist. By rapping and listening, anywhere that could shelter an intruder would likely be revealed."

"But no such place was found." Holmes finished. "Thank you, Watson. Now I have done all I can to ensure our privacy, save locking the door. Perhaps you would attend to that."

I crossed the room to turn the key and returned to my chair. We gave Holmes our full attention as he spoke quietly of his intentions.

"Tomorrow morning I shall again visit Armington Magna. There I will visit the post office to send a telegram, confiding at the same time that one of Miss Monkton's relatives has died in Cornwall. Spreading this news should present no problem, if the postmistress's reputation as a gossip is well earned. Naturally Miss

Monkton will wish to return home immediately, and Watson will accompany her to the station in time for the mid-morning train. He will help her aboard, and she will depart."

Turville nodded. "But, in keeping with what you have revealed to me, it will actually be Lady Heminworth who leaves?"

"Quite so. Doubtlessly, her Ladyship still has the hat and veil she wore at the funerals of her husband and son. That is the sort of thing that Miss Monkton, returning home in mourning, would be expected to wear. The substitution should be difficult to detect, especially from a distance."

"But how do I take charge of my patient, unobserved?"

"You, Dr. Turville, will board the train at Claverton, the station it will pass through immediately before Armington Magna. When Watson puts your patient aboard, you will be but a few feet away." Holmes hesitated. "Accordingly, while awaiting the train on the platform, and for as long as possible after boarding, her Ladyship must be discouraged from speaking."

"I will try to ensure this."

"Excellent! When this is done, the issues that remain are the protection of Miss Monkton, and her adoption of the role of her aunt. The servants will be told that it is on medical advice that Lady Heminworth is to be isolated in her bedchamber. Dr Watson or I will be present and armed at all times."

"Congratulations, Holmes," I applauded. "You seem to have thought of everything."

"When I find myself believing that," my friend smiled, "I know it is time to redouble my scrutiny of my plans. Many of my past opponents now reside in prison because they were convinced their schemes were flawless."

"And so we all have our parts to play," Miss Monkton said. "I pray that we will be successful."

"Take heart," I advised. "It may be as well to instruct one of the maids to pack your travelling case, as soon as Holmes returns. You must appear to be grieved and, it occurs to me, her Ladyship's rings must be removed from her fingers and exchanged with yours."

Holmes beamed. "Watson, you go from strength to strength. I have said that we must not underestimate our enemy again, so nothing must be left to chance."

"Shoes, then," Turville suggested to Miss Monkton. "Lady Heminworth must wear a pair of yours."

"That will present no difficulty, since we are of the same size."

Our discussion continued until late, when Holmes pronounced himself satisfied. We then retired, each well prepared for tomorrow but still concerned for Lady Heminworth and mindful of the threat of our enemy's presence.

Immediately after breakfast, Turville and I conducted a further examination of Lady Heminworth. There seemed little change, but my colleague seemed pleased and full of enthusiasm for his part in our plan.

Presently, Holmes returned from Armington Magna, saying nothing of his activities there. Walters was told by Miss Monkton of the death of an uncle, which necessitated her return to Cornwall. I confess to thinking that the theatrical profession was the poorer for her absence, for tears shone in her eyes as she instructed the butler as to her imminent departure.

Holmes thoughtfully paced the Great Hall until the time arrived for Turville to leave for Claverton station, on the pretext that we had arranged. We shook his hand and bade him farewell.

"I find your friend to be a most excellent fellow, Watson." Holmes remarked as the brougham sped away. "I am certain that Lady Heminworth could not be in better hands."

163

"I am glad you approve of him. Walters should be able to drive back here in plenty of time, I think."

He nodded. "Miss Monkton will have her Ladyship prepared by then. I went to see Sergeant Grimes earlier, and called in at several places from where news of our little fiction will surely spread quickly."

"I hope our enemy is convinced, Holmes."

"The only weak point in our plan is the leaving of Miss Monkton at Theobald Grange while we are at the station. She suggested leaving Walters, or even Grover, as an armed sentry outside her Ladyship's room, but given the cunning of our adversary I consider this would be the most unforgivable folly."

"No doubt you intend to stay yourself. I would agree that to be for the best."

"You anticipate me, Watson. But let us go into the house, there may be something we can do to enhance the proceedings."

Miss Monkton met us in the Great Hall, looking apprehensive now that the time had come for her to play her part.

"All is ready," she said. "I wait only for the signal to begin."

Holmes consulted his pocket watch. "The time has come. Dr Watson will attend her Ladyship in fifteen minutes."

She left us and climbed the stairs rather hurriedly. Holmes said little while we waited, getting up from his chair once to look from the window in the direction of Maybell Wood. When the time had elapsed, I took my bag to Lady Heminworth's bedchamber.

I had discussed with Turville the advisability of administering a mild sedative to his patient, to reduce the risk of her revealing all by an unguarded movement or spoken word. He had assured me that this was unnecessary, in her present emotional state, and I saw clearly now that he was right.

Lady Heminworth sat near her bed in a dark costume that was unmistakeably that of a younger woman. Her pleasant smile was unaltered, but she did not acknowledge my entrance by the slightest movement and seemed only dimly aware of the presence of her niece.

Miss Monkton had dressed normally, as she would not be seen out of this room. As I watched, she placed a black wide-brimmed hat with a dark veil upon her Ladyship's head. After a moment, she carefully helped her aunt to her feet.

"I have done all that I can, doctor. I pray that it goes well, for it was I who suggested this to Mr Holmes."

"Had he not had confidence in it, he would never have allowed your plan to proceed," I assured her. "I am certain all will be well, provided no one is allowed to approach her."

She looked around anxiously. "Where is Mr Holmes to be while this is done?"

"He will be close by, never fear."

"Near to this room?"

"We have sworn to protect you, especially now."

Presently the brougham returned. I heard Holmes' quick strides as he crossed the great hall to open the door. A few words were exchanged with Walters, and then my friend's voice reached me from below.

"Watson, it is time for you to go."

Her Ladyship rose immediately, as if dimly aware of what was taking place. Miss Monkton threw her arms around her, explaining in most affectionate terms that this parting was but temporary and for the sake of her well-being and protection. This farewell was without acknowledgment and quickly over, and I gently guided Lady Heminworth from the room.

The chamber door closed behind us, and we met Holmes at the top of the staircase.

"I have ensured that Walters and the maids will remain in the kitchen." he said. "They have been told that Miss Monkton wishes to depart quietly, without ceremony, because of the intensity of her grief."

"That is as well."

He took out his pocket watch. "The horse is still fresh, and you have ample time to reach the station. It is unlikely you will need it, but keep your revolver ready. As for myself, I prevailed upon Sergeant Grimes to lend me a pistol from the official armoury. Until your return, I will remain outside this room to serve our charge as necessary."

"I will be back here before one o'clock." I predicted.

"Take particular care when handing over the brougham to Rawlings. He must suspect nothing." Holmes confronted Lady Heminworth with a little bow. "Goodbye, Your Ladyship. I look forward to hearing of your return to good health."

The veil prevented us from seeing any sign of understanding she might have given. I guided her down the stairs and we boarded the carriage. In moments the house was behind us, as the horse set off at a fast trot.

I slowed the horse when we reached the road. We rode in silence, except for my occasional words of encouragement. Lady Heminworth sat statue-like, now and then moving her head. Surrounded by the rural landscape our situation seemed to me unreal. I felt trapped in some morbid dream, as we wound our way through the quiet lanes.

From not far off, I heard a trumpet and the shouts of riders. Over a hedgerow I saw red-coated huntsmen following the hounds, after a fox that was proving too cunning and too quick for them. Drawing nearer I acknowledged the waves of several locals who recognised the brougham, and before long we found ourselves in the little road beside Armington Magna station.

With the horse tethered, I helped her Ladyship down. I was thankful for that day without wind, for it was unlikely that the veil would be blown aside. With care I guided her into the station, speaking reassuringly but not addressing her by name.

The train arrived precisely on time. We stood back as a group of farmers and labourers alighted, then those waiting on the platform climbed aboard and seated themselves before the smiling face of Turville appeared in the doorway.

"We will be on the Brighton express within an hour or two," he said as I assisted Lady Heminworth up the steps. "Goodbye, Watson. You will hear from me."

I saw that they were settled in a half-empty coach before the train pulled away. It disappeared down the line leaving a long plume of smoke that began to disperse before I left the platform. Outside, the horse waited patiently, nibbling on a patch of grass beside the station entrance. I again took the reins, now urging the animal on in my eagerness to re-join Holmes. My friend's assurance that the end of this curious affair was upon us filled me with anticipation, and whatever it held we would face it together as in all our previous adventures.

My prediction as to time proved correct. I had given charge of the brougham to Rawlings, without incident, and was once more seated in the great hall, well before the hour of one o'clock.

"I have told Walters that some cold beef will be sufficient for luncheon, if you approve." Holmes explained.

"As far as I am concerned, it is enough."

"I have also mentioned that her Ladyship wishes to take her meals in her room for the present, and they are to be served by you only at the times when you look in on her."

"And how did he take that?"

167

"With a faint air of disapproval," my friend said with some amusement. "Miss Monkton and I agreed upon it to avert any suspicions he may have formed. I remained outside her door until I heard the carriage returning, and she is aware that she has only to call out to bring us to her instantly."

"Everything seems in hand for the moment," I observed. "Miss Monkton seems to be standing well against all this."

"She is unsettled by being confined to her aunt's bedchamber and naturally anxious for things to return to normal."

Walters brought the beef and set it on the table. I carved a portion and took it up to Miss Monkton, together with some vegetables and bread, while Holmes took his share. She gratefully received it, remarking that her appetite was much improved by the knowledge that her aunt was safe, despite the threat that remained over us here. When I had satisfied myself as to her comfort, and reminded her to call us at the slightest suggestion of our adversary's presence, I re-joined my friend.

Holmes rarely eats while his mind wrestles with an unsolved problem. His attacks on the roast beef however, convinced me at once of his mastery of the situation, and his uncharacteristic enjoyment of his food gave me yet more confidence.

Walters brought coffee, and I was sorry to see his troubled expression.

"Time will heal Miss Monkton's loss," I assured him. "The sad fact is that each of us must die in his due time, but it is certain her uncle has gone to a better place. She will return as soon as her grief has passed."

For a moment he stared at me blankly, and I realised that I had misunderstood.

"Oh, yes, I see, sir. I am sure that will be so." He said uncertainly.

Holmes" interest sharpened. "Something has happened. There are scratches on your hands, Walters. Who have you struggled with?"

The butler lowered his eyes, looking more concerned than ever. "I had to restrain one of the maids, sir. She became hysterical."

"What was the cause?" I asked.

"I sent her to the village, to get something for the kitchen. She found the place in uproar. She was terrified."

"But why?"

"A stranger to the village, an elderly woman, was found strangled near the railway station. Her body is thought to have lain hidden for two or three days."

"A victim of robbers, perhaps?" Holmes enquired.

"No sir, money was left on her person."

"Most curious, but that does not rule out robbery entirely. The thief may have been disturbed."

"Begging your pardon, sirs," Walters said. "I have just remembered something. The letter destroyed by Mr Rawlings was posted in Kent, and Sergeant Grimes has evidence that this woman came from there also. Perhaps there is a connection."

Holmes gave me a grim look "I cannot recall such an incident."

"It occurred in your absence, sir." The butler frowned. "You were in London, I believe."

"Ah. Yes, of course."

Walters left us before Holmes spoke again, with a despairing hand on his brow.

"Why did you not tell me of this immediately upon my return, Watson? The postmark on that letter was vital to my investigation."

My spirits plummeted. I had never before felt as sad or inadequate in our association as at that instant. Worse, I prayed that my forgetfulness had not somehow cost that poor woman her life.

Holmes understood my thoughts, and his expression softened. "Perhaps, after all, this is an unrelated incident. Or our enemy knew of the unfortunate woman's impending arrival, whereas we did not. Cheer up, old fellow."

"No, there can be no excuse, Holmes. How can I make amends?" A thought struck me. "If I had shot that fiend last night, from the window, perhaps she would be alive still!"

Holmes shook his head. "Did you not hear Walters say that the body had lain concealed for two or three days? No, Watson, the blame for this cannot be laid at your door." He stopped abruptly. "Ah, but I hear a bicycle being propped against the wall and an uncertain step approaching the door. The village postmaster has been as good as his promise to send the replies to my telegrams here immediately they arrive."

With that he rose and strode to the door. Walters appeared but retreated at a sign from me, and I heard the clink of coins before the telegram-boy rode away.

Holmes returned and seated himself opposite me. As he tore open the envelope I tried to read in his face something of what he read. His mouth set in a stern line, but his eyes glittered with excitement. This was familiar to me: The chase would soon begin!

Disappointingly, Holmes said nothing but sank into one of his thoughtful silences. I went to the window and looked out at Maybell Wood, where the late afternoon sun shone brightly on the dense trees. Perhaps they concealed our enemy at this moment, as he plotted the end of the woman he had so mercilessly taunted.

"Tomorrow morning," Holmes said suddenly, intruding upon my thoughts, "the jester will be dead or in the hands of the police, as will his accomplice. That is, of course, unless they are able to overcome both you and myself."

"How can you be certain, as to the time?"

"Because I have arranged it so."

I could not imagine how this could be. "Please explain yourself, Holmes."

"Gladly, although the strategy is simplicity itself. However, to avoid unnecessary repetition, let us repair to Lady Heminworth's room, where I will describe what is likely to take place."

"I am very glad of your company," Miss Monkton said after admitting us and locking the door. "Confinement is not easy for me."

"Take courage, it will soon be over." Holmes told her. "By tomorrow morning, if all goes well, your endurance should be at an end."

I noticed that he spoke quietly, as he had to me downstairs. Now, he stopped abruptly and commenced walking around the perimeter of the room, rapping on the panelling as he had previously in the Great Hall.

"Do you know of any secret entrances or hidden compartments anywhere in this chamber?" he asked Miss Monkton.

"As you surmised before, this house is probably full of such places but they are very old, and probably some are no longer usable. No one remembers their whereabouts."

"Yet there must be something of the sort, since the jester was able to place Cairn's severed hand on her Ladyship's pillow without attracting attention. This is a large room, so if we move our chairs to the centre and speak quietly, as before, we should not be overheard."

171

When this was done, Miss Monkton turned to Holmes eagerly. "How can you know what will take place? What is to happen?"

"Now that your aunt is safely away from here, we can force the pace of events." He leaned forward in his chair in a conspiratorial fashion. "Whilst in the village this morning, I let it be known that a company of Scotland Yard men will be arriving at Theobald Grange tomorrow. I advised Walters similarly."

"Against such numbers, the jester will be overwhelmed!" she exclaimed.

"It is unlike you, Holmes, to ask Lestrade for assistance." I said suspiciously.

"In fact, Scotland Yard was instrumental in supplying information about our adversary's motives. However, Watson, I understand your reluctance to believe that I have actually requested their help at the conclusion of this case." He took out his pipe, then uncharacteristically decided against smoking and returned it to his pocket. "Although, you will remember that I have done this before."

"Then Scotland Yard will be visiting us?"

"Not before this is over."

Miss Monkton's puzzled look left her face suddenly. "All is clear to me, Mr Holmes. The jester, believing that many more will arrive tomorrow to oppose him, will seize his last opportunity and strike tonight."

"Precisely."

"And we will be ready," I said.

Holmes nodded. "We will, but again we must take every precaution. This is a cunning and murderous enemy who could yet get the better of us."

"Please God, no." Miss Monkton said.

My friend smiled. "Let us hope that He has decided the matter in our favour."

Presently the chamber darkened, and Holmes and I lit the lamps ourselves. We heard Walters drawing the curtains and attending to the illumination of the Great Hall below, and I went downstairs to bring back a tray of food.

"It is a strange feeling, being the bait in a trap," Miss Monkton said when the three of us were together again.

"To be afraid is understandable," Holmes said gently, "but there is still time to withdraw, if you wish it. In any event, Dr Watson and I are here for your protection."

She smiled graciously. "I know I am in safe hands. I truly believe that there is no one who could have done more for my aunt and myself than you gentlemen. But I, too, have vowed that I will do all I can to bring her tormentor to justice. I cannot turn aside from it."

"Bravo!" I exclaimed.

"Please tell me if there is anything more you require of me. I am at your disposal."

Holmes looked across at her quickly. "Can you tell us, now that your aunt is safe, the reason for Donald Heminworth's banishment from this house?"

Miss Monkton glanced at us both, uncertainly. "I have never been told of course, but certain things became clear to me from chance remarks between my uncle and aunt, shortly after Donald's visit. They never intended it, but it would have been difficult to avoid overhearing."

"Pray tell us what was said."

She hesitated, trying to remember. "We were all surprised when Donald returned from South Africa, for he appeared without warning. I recall that both parents were overjoyed, for not only had their son returned, but he had brought with him something that would assure the future of the Heminworth family. The nature of this was never explained to me, but I know it must have been something of great value, for my uncle said several times that the end of the decline of the past few years was now certain. Shortly afterwards, the sudden argument between father and son resulted in the banishment. I was never able to learn more."

Holmes sat for some minutes with his head upon his chest.

"I believe I have it now, Watson." His face grew keen and shone with triumph. "And so, my case is complete!"

I was about to congratulate him, and I saw that Miss Monkton had many questions, but he forestalled us with a raised hand.

"There will be ample time for explanations when this night is over. Whether the jester intends to kill Lady Heminworth, I am unsure, for it would suit his purpose equally well to drive her mad. His object is to gain possession of the Eye of Africa, the fabulous gem that your cousin brought to England to restore his family's name. If her ladyship cannot be forced to tell him of its hiding place, then he hopes to cause such concern for her health that Donald Heminworth will return here, to be induced to give up the jewel for the sake of his mother's life or sanity. From this I must conclude that your cousin is residing in a place much nearer to us than Australia."

"That plan is monstrous, Holmes." I retorted.

"I cannot imagine where Donald can be," Miss Monkton said thoughtfully. "My uncle always spoke of Australia."

"Possibly he foresaw the need to hide his son's whereabouts, in anticipation of a situation such as we find ourselves in," Holmes speculated. "But no matter, your cousin has no part to play in the events ahead of us."

"It is fully dark now," I observed.

174

Holmes cast a glance to the window. "The jester could strike at any time now. If you both follow my instructions exactly, we will succeed. Miss Monkton, you must on no account leave this room until either Dr Watson or myself comes for you. I doubt that you will sleep, or be able to read, but your lamp must be kept burning. I have already ensured that the wick and oil are sufficient to last the night. Watson will be stationed outside your door with his revolver, and will give chase only if our enemy is actually within his sight."

"You said there is probably more than one against us," I reminded him.

A brief smile crossed his lips. "I had not forgotten. It is because of that that I must leave you, yet I will not be far off."

The evening wore on and we spent more time in discussion, I think because, like myself, Holmes wished Miss Monkton's time of waiting to be short. She tried bravely to hide her fear, and showed little sign of it when the time came for Holmes and I to leave the chamber.

"That chair is hard and upright," he told me, "you will find it difficult to fall asleep. Place it in front of the door, and keep your revolver ready. I look forward to seeing you both in the morning, when this is all behind us."

With that he turned and left, his boots echoing along the corridor and on the stairs. Presently the door of the main entrance closed solidly, and I looked down from the window as he strode away from the house. His hat was firmly on his head, and his ulster billowed out behind him like the wings of some great bird, until the darkness finally hid him. I knew not where he was bound, only that he would meet our enemy, somewhere in the night.

Chapter Eleven - The Phantom of Maybell Wood

I stared out from the corridor into the darkness, seeing nothing but the faint glow from the downstairs windows. After a while even that vanished, probably because the oil in the lamps was spent. Walters had been instructed to remain in his quarters until morning.

Then began a lonely and silent vigil such I had known only once before. On that occasion Holmes and I waited together for death to enter the room soundlessly. Perhaps I now faced a similar situation alone.

The only light now came from under the door of her Ladyship's room, and from the pipe I smoked silently. For a while my mind wandered once more over the curious aspects of this affair, and I confess to much concern regarding its outcome and the welfare of Miss Monkton and Holmes.

Once or twice I heard movements in the room behind me and I strained my ears to catch any cry of alarm, but there was nothing. More than once sleep almost claimed me, so that I was obliged to shake my head and sit straighter in the unyielding chair.

Time passed with interminable slowness. I had no means of measurement; my pocket watch was useless without light and there was no chiming clock to mark off the hours.

I got to my feet and strode back to the window to stave off cramp. The ancient floorboards creaked with every movement and I stopped to listen for similar sounds from elsewhere in the house, but I heard none.

Keeping my hand on my revolver I looked out once more. Now I could make out the wings of the house, like an embracing arm on each side, faintly through the blackness. I turned my attention to the heavens. Myriads of stars shone down from a clear sky, all dwarfed by the full moon, and I realised that this illumination meant I could after all see the numbers of my watch. I took it from my waistcoat pocket and opened the cover, inclining the face towards the window. It showed the time to be almost five o'clock!

A further two or three hours and the night would have passed uneventfully. Dawn would rob this house of its spectral qualities, and the jester's last chance (as he must perceive it) would be gone.

I returned to my chair. After listening to the silence for a while more, my thoughts settled on things dear and familiar to me: Mary, my dear wife; Baker Street; Mrs Hudson, and others. I smiled in the darkness at the memory of the scruffy band of urchins, referred to by Holmes as his Irregulars, who had been so useful in some of his cases, and wondered if we would indeed find ourselves back in London soon, with this affair behind us.

Something alerted me. I stood up warily, my weapon held at my side. Through the window the sky grew lighter as I watched. Then the impossibility of it struck me. It was not yet time for dawn, at this time of year. This could not be natural light! I pressed my face to the glass, but the west wing obstructed my view. A fierce glow flickered further off, and a shower of sparks floated on the breeze. Then the brougham came tearing across the courtyard, and the urgent cries of Miss Monkton rang in my ears.

"Doctor. Doctor Watson, the stables are afire. I can see the blaze from my window!"

I watched as the coach disappeared. "Calm yourself, please. Walters has gone for help."

"But the horses, I can hear their cries."

"How many are there?"

"Three. They will be burned to death."

"No. One is harnessed to the coach and the others are loose. They are terrified but too far from the blaze to be in danger. I can see them near Maybell Wood."

"Thank God the poor creatures are safe." Her voice was louder now; she stood nearer to the door. "What can have happened?"

"This is a diversion, meant to occupy our attention while our enemy makes his way into the house. We are prepared. Remain watchful and summon me immediately anything occurs."

She said something more, but my attention had been drawn away by movement from below. Shortly after, a stair creaked under a cautious foot.

My revolver was a reassuring weight in my hand. I began to consider that the sound had been imaginary, or the settling of the timbers of this old house, when it was repeated. This time there was no mistaking it, and again. Now the intruder grew bolder, climbing three steps before pausing to listen. He would be expecting to find us unprepared, but my finger was already on the trigger and my aim fixed on the top of the staircase.

But could this be Holmes? Perhaps my friend had returned, satisfied that there was nothing to be done this night. I remembered a similar thought before I encountered the jester in the wine cellar. Decidedly, this could not be, for if it were Holmes, then why did he not call out?

No, the footsteps that had now reached the landing were not those of my friend, but of our adversary. Slowly I rose, thankful that the chair made no sound.

To my shame, and despite my firearm, I felt a fearful compulsion to turn and run. I was familiar with this sensation from my experiences in the Afghan campaign, and knew how to dispel it by summoning my reserves of courage. It came to mind that Holmes might be dead or injured if our enemy had broken through his protection and entered the house unhindered, and I thrust the thought away. For fear of revealing my position I did not call upon the intruder to identify himself, but remained silent as the footfalls continued along the corridor. Only the moonbeams slanting in from the window, and the faint light from the fire, relieved the pitch darkness.

I strained my eyes to see as a shape detached itself from the deep shadows, moving slowly and carrying something with both hands. The figure took two or three more steps and was still. It had seen me. In the faint moonlight it appeared as something shapeless, a half-illuminated thing that was at once deadly and ridiculous. I stood directly in front of the bedchamber door that would be Miss Monkton's only protection if I failed her, and raised my revolver. The figure moved with the speed of a striking snake, and I instinctively threw myself to one side as something struck the panelling with a splitting crash. I struggled to my feet, having lost my pistol in the darkness, and the jester emerged from the gloom shrieking with the maniacal laughter we had heard before. He moved with incredible speed in a curious dance, so that each movement brought him nearer. The meagre light glittered on the long knife or sword he held. He slashed in all directions, the air hissing as during a dervish ritual, while in his madness repeating a single word: "DEATH! DEATH! DEATH! DEATH!"

Beside me a long lance which I recognised from the display of medieval weaponry in the Great Hall, quivered in the wooden panelling. It came to me that my only defence might lie with this and I seized the shaft, but all my strength could not dislodge it and the jester was almost upon me. Miss Monkton's terrified screams were drowned by his shrieks, and that hideous mask seemed to float before me. Again I retreated out of his reach, the swinging blade narrowly missing my head and embedding itself in the door. I tried to find some heavy object to use as a weapon, but I stumbled against the overturned chair. The jester screamed, wrenching the blade free and wielding it like an executioner's axe to embed it where I had lain a moment before. His cries turned to curses as he tried unsuccessfully to wrest the weapon from the floor. When it was freed I would certainly die, for he would not miss again.

He shrieked in triumph as the blade tore from the wood. I managed to get to my knees, and in my frantic efforts to stand brushed my hand against something solid. I searched the floor

179

around me desperately. If this were an object of sufficient weight, perhaps one of the small bronze sculptures that had been overturned, I might delay him with an accurate throw.

Then it was in my grasp. It was not a sculpture; it was my pistol!

Even then he could have brought about my end before I was able to aim. But he paused to laugh at me, to pour obscene blasphemies into my face, and that was his undoing. I fired twice, the first shot missing despite the closeness of the target, and I heard a window shatter before I fired again. Immediately his cries became different, full of surprise and pain as he crashed to the floor.

"He is down, and I am unharmed!" I shouted to calm Miss Monkton's fears.

But I moved slowly like a man afflicted with fever, pulling myself to my feet by gripping the door handle with my free hand. The jester still lived, groaning and clutching his side with bloodied fingers. Breathlessly, I aimed my pistol, but Holmes" remark about cheating the hangman came to me and I took my finger from the trigger. I would not burden my conscience with his death, but I would see him in the hands of the police within the hour.

Dawn approached; the blackness outside had given way to grey. The jester lay still, propped against the wall with one side of his costume stained with blood. I noticed that the bells were missing from his sleeves, probably he had removed them in order to enter the house and climb the stairs silently. Odd, I thought, that such a fiend should clothe himself in the garments of a figure of mirth and gaiety.

He staggered to his feet, watching me and maintaining his balance by leaning against the wall. In the poor light, I saw that he left a bloody handprint.

"Remain still," I warned him. "If you give me reason, I will not hesitate to fire."

"I mean to recover what is mine," he hissed from behind the mask. "I will kill you all, if I must."

"Dr Watson, what is happening?"

Miss Monkton's terrified voice, coming suddenly from the locked chamber, startled me. My attention was distracted for no more than an instant, but for my prisoner it was enough. I sensed his quick movement as he threw something that passed close to my face and pierced the far wall. Then he was gone, and had already reached the head of the stairs when I fired. He toppled forward, struggling to regain his balance. At the foot of the stairs he ran, but the sounds ceased abruptly. I knew then that he would leave the house as secretly as he entered and that, despite appearances, his injuries were not serious. From the top of the staircase, I saw that only shadows now filled the Great Hall.

Wearily, but thankful that no harm had come to Miss Monkton, I made my way back. I paused to inspect the woodwork, where it held the object thrown by the jester to effect his escape. It appeared to be a small iron ball covered in spikes. After a quick examination, made difficult by the dim light, I identified it as part of a mediaeval weapon known as a morning star, or mace-and-chain, where such a ball would be wielded at the end of a chain attached to a handle. This, I knew, was used long ago in hand-to-hand fighting, but by its rusty condition was unlikely to be from the collection adorning the walls below.

I turned away and unlocked the chamber door. Miss Monkton stood near the dressing table, her face white in the dull gleam from the window.

"Dr Watson!" She cried. "Thank God. Are you injured?"

"I am merely bruised," I assured her. "The darkness made his aim more difficult, as it did mine. He escaped, but not without wounds. His blood is on the floor and on the stairs."

"And Mr Holmes?"

"He is still outside. I have not seen him since he left."

"Please God he, too, is safe," she said in an unsteady voice. "I must see the servants. The gunfire will have alarmed them."

I went to the window that had been broken by my stray shot. The breaking dawn had softened the shadows so that I saw the jester limping for the shelter of the trees. He appeared now as a slightly bedraggled figure, little troubled by his wounds. To bring him down from here would have been difficult, the range was too great for an accurate shot, but I determined that he should not escape.

I have no memory of running and leaping down the stairs, but I found myself tearing at the fastenings of the main door moments later. With the bolts drawn I paused, realising that my efforts were useless without the key. Then Walters appeared beside me.

"Sir," he began, "Miss Monkton said...."

"Never mind," I shouted in frustration, "help me with this door!"

"But the gunfire, I thought...."

"The key!" I fumed. "Have you got it?"

He produced it and fumbled with the lock.

"Hurry! The jester is getting away."

The door opened and I seized it from him, throwing it wide. Gripping my revolver I ran headlong into Maybell Wood, just as the first rays of the sun broke through.

I entered the trees. Suddenly there was only silence and stillness. He had vanished, his lurid costume lost among the greens and browns surrounding me. I stopped after a few steps, listening for direction. At first all remained quiet, then the cries of disturbed birds attracted my attention. I made off through the ancient trunks and branches until I came to a path, which soon led to a clearing. I recognised the place where Holmes and I had first seen the jester disappear, but now I faced the opposite direction.

I stood still, my eyes and ears straining for some sign of him. Then a movement, a flickering of light, made me turn to the cluster of large oaks ahead. He was up there as before, now flying quickly from tree to tree and making his escape as I watched. But not this time, I vowed. I brought up my revolver and aimed. I could not fail to bring him down. My finger tightened on the trigger.

"That would be a waste of perfectly good ammunition, Watson." Sherlock Holmes said from beside me.

"In heaven's name, Holmes!"

He laughed at my surprise. "Put down your pistol, old fellow. His image will be gone in an instant."

His words were proven at once, for the apparition vanished.

"But I could have brought an end to this dreadful business. Surely there is proof enough now, even for Scotland Yard?"

He nodded. "There is abundant proof, but I fear you are in error. Your target practice would have solved nothing."

Confused, I was about to ask many questions, but he held up a hand for silence. We shaded our eyes from a brilliant shaft of early sunlight illuminating the clearing from behind us.

"This place is perfectly positioned," he observed. "He chose it well."

"As I recall, it was the same when we were here before, but of course the evening sun shone from the opposite direction."

"Precisely. I think that you too, Watson, are well on the way to discovering the secret of the jester's flight."

"Holmes, I am as much in the dark as ever."

"No matter," he smiled briefly. "Everything will soon be clear. Keep your revolver ready. This way."

183

We trod stealthily, taking care to avoid fallen twigs or bushes that would rustle or snap. Abruptly, he placed a finger on his lips to indicate again the need for silence, before pausing to examine a thin sapling. I saw a smear of fresh blood and Holmes' eyes glittered with satisfaction as we crept deeper into the wood.

"The last act is about to be played, I think." He said in a whisper.

"But Holmes, he flew in the opposite direction."

He shook his head. "Look."

I raised my eyes to see the evil mask of the jester, looking down from the branches of a half-dead tree. Instantly, the strong arm of my friend pulled me into concealment as the blast of a heavy-gauge shotgun ripped past us.

Lying in the damp undergrowth, I turned my head slowly to face Holmes, but he was nowhere to be seen. I looked up to see the jester still perched in the tree with his shotgun held ready. He sensed my movement and stopped, to bring up his weapon. I still had my revolver but no protection, and he had already aimed. The click of the hammer being cocked came to me clearly. He had set his weapon in the fork of a heavy bough, but a thick branch thrown by Holmes struck his face an instant before he fired. The charge tore into the tree nearest to me, three or four feet above my head, as the jester cried out and fell heavily to the ground.

I was on him even before Holmes, with my revolver pressed to his head, but there was no need. He lay insensible, and I tore off the mask.

"It is Rawlings, as you suspected."

Holmes nodded. "There were few other possibilities."

"The man has the look of a wild beast, even while unconscious."

"His madness is of the most dangerous and criminal kind. Let us make sure he can do no more harm." He whipped a pair of police handcuffs from his pocket and secured our prisoner's hands across his back. "Attend to his wounds, Watson, as best you can, so that he is in good health when he mounts the scaffold."

"He will heal," I said in a moment.

"Take the scarf from his neck and secure his legs tightly, we do not want him wandering off while we complete our task."

As I did this I reflected that my friend had been right in saying that the jester was not alone. Rawlings was a thickset, heavy man, quite unlike the jester who performed the acrobatics we had witnessed. Also, it could not have been Rawlings who attacked me in the wine cellar, as I met him a moment after watching the jester disappear into the distance.

I tied the twisted scarf tightly, pulling hard on the knot. "I cannot see him getting free without help."

Holmes turned his head to look towards the trees where the jester had flown.

"That is where we must look."

He led me to a thick clump of bushes, not far out of the clearing. I noticed that he also held a revolver in readiness. We pushed through a gap in the thorny hedge and saw at once a small man, almost a dwarf, dismantling some sort of equipment. He must have been awaiting Rawlings' return, for an angry expression of surprise and disbelief crossed his face when he saw us. He dropped the glass vessel he held, then recovered himself and ran.

"Stop," Holmes shouted, "or we fire!"

He obeyed, but when he turned to face us I saw a curved dagger in his hand. Deliberately, he aimed and threw it at Holmes in a single fast movement and I saw my friend fall. I shot twice but my target moved too quickly. Beyond the bushes the land rose at the edge of the wood, and I saw him framed for an instant against

185

the morning sky. He ignored my command to halt and hurled a large stone towards me. It struck a tree less than a foot from my face, but then I fired again and did not miss.

His body fell across the roots of a great oak but I ignored him, for I was anxious about Holmes. I turned to him and felt relief at once, for he had gotten to his feet. As I watched he withdrew the dagger and threw it down.

"I really must compliment my tailor on the quality of his cloth," he said, sitting down with his back against a tree. "A less substantial coat would have allowed greater penetration, possibly with fatal results. As it is, the point no more than grazed my flesh, and I believe I have stopped the blood flow already with my handkerchief."

"Nevertheless, I must inspect the wound."

He sighed. "If you must, Watson, but I find the prospect of inspecting the body of the jester's accomplice far more interesting."

I was glad to find little damage. Holmes had indeed stemmed the bleeding. The wound was shallow, and no more than the application of some soothing ointment and a dressing would be necessary for later.

Impatiently, he struggled to his feet the instant I concluded my examination. Together, we made our way to where our enemy had fallen. He lay on his back, covered with blood.

"He still lives," I observed with surprise.

"Take care, Watson, he is as much a murderer as Rawlings."

The man before us trembled and groaned. His eyes opened and fixed us with a painful stare.

"Don't move," I advised. "I will do what I can for you."

"Too late," he gasped. "My time has come. I should never have left the air."

I kneeled to loosen his collar, but his eyes took on a blank stillness and I knew he was dead.

In a moment I stood beside my friend again. "What did he mean, Holmes?"

He gestured towards the body. "All will be clear to you, when I introduce Mr Fergus Farraday."

"The aerialist? From Mr Zamil's circus?"

"The same, who appeared as the jester when somersaults and other acrobatics were required. Also the murderer of the Russian, Barcherov, and, of course, of Cairns and Blackthorne."

I shook my head in perplexity, there was still much that puzzled me, and one thing in particular.

"Holmes, I know you will explain everything when you are ready, but for now I would be obliged if you would tell me how this man flew and disappeared."

"He did that, yet he was here when we came upon him, only moments later." He smiled artfully. "A truly singular feature of this case, wouldn't you say, Watson?"

"Indeed. But did you discover how it was done?"

My friend led me to the place where we had first set eyes on Farraday. He showed me a wooden chest and a metal box with coloured lenses set in its sides.

"Why, it is a magic lantern."

"Certainly, it is a device based on the same principle," Holmes confirmed.

"And is that a mirror?"

He picked up some fragments of the glass dropped by Farraday. "It is actually the remains of a reflector. This metal box holds the condensing lens, the light aperture and the double convex lens. The apparatus is portable and fits into the wooden chest.

187

Rawlings or Farraday operated it, or appeared in costume, as necessary to their plan."

"Did you suspect this?"

"Not at first. I was certain only that no supernatural element existed here, other than in Lady Heminworth's imagination. When we first saw the jester fly through the trees, I was puzzled by his indistinct appearance, even in the poor light. Then the significance of the timing struck me."

I considered this, and then it came to me. "It is connected with this place, for the jester has disappeared nowhere else. After the incident in the wine cellar, he simply faded into the distance, normally. Every morning from the east, a ray of sunlight strikes this spot exactly. A similar effect occurs from the west, at sunset."

"Bravo, Watson!" said Holmes good-naturedly. "It is only just past dawn and already you excel yourself! Indeed, our escaping jester was no more than a projected image, illuminated by the rising or setting sun. All that was required to produce the illusion of his movement was the slow turning of this handle to rotate the beam. A cut-out paper shape provided the silhouette."

"So that was why the jester never appeared on cloudy days! When we pursued him before, he must have been concealed a few feet away as we watched his image escape through the trees."

"Which he did after his torment of Lady Heminworth. Now, Watson, if you will be good enough to cover the body of that blackguard with this coat that he left so untidily, after first removing his belt, we will let Sergeant Grimes know where he is to be found, presently."

Why Holmes wanted the belt I could not guess, but remembering that he was rarely without purpose, I obeyed. We strolled unconcernedly back to Rawlings, through trees that held no more danger, with Holmes in that cheerful mood that often settled upon him at the conclusion of an adventure, when all is well again.

"Ah, but I see that the jester has awakened," he said on sighting the writhing figure among the bluebells. "No, Rawlings, or whatever your name truly is, your curses and obscenities will avail you nothing with us. Watson, see if you can wipe some of the blood from his face, he should be at least presentable when the police arrive at the house. I see that my rather fortunate aim with that branch caused some little damage."

I did this with difficulty, for I had to avoid teeth that snapped like those of a wild beast. Throughout, Rawlings continued to pour out a profusion of oaths.

"What are we to do with him?" I asked Holmes.

"I do not think it wise or necessary to allow him unrestricted movement. When I make you aware of his past, Watson, you will not fail to agree. I see that he wears braces so the removal of his belt will cause little inconvenience. Attach it to that of Farraday, and we have an improvised pair of leg-irons. Cut away the scarf and he will be able to walk, but not to lengthen his stride as he would to run. I suggest you close your ears to the accompaniment that he will doubtless provide, and concentrate your imagination instead upon the pleasure it will give us to tell Miss Monkton that all danger is past."

"That will make an excellent conversation piece at breakfast," I said as I set about my task.

To the best of my recollection, during the time it took to return to Theobald Grange, both Sherlock Holmes and I spoke but little as we watched our prisoner carefully.

"The brougham has been left at the door, I see. Walters has returned with the fire brigade." he said as we approached. "The poor fellow will have to go straight back to the village for the police, if he has not had the wit to summon them already. As you must have seen, I released the horses from the blazing stable, where they had been abandoned to their fate. No doubt Grover will be sent to gather them together, before they are sheltered elsewhere."

"The poor creatures must have been terrified. Let us hope they are none the worse for their experience."

My friend nodded. "In order to reduce our further involvement, I will write a telegram to Lestrade for Walters to send on his return to the village. For the same reason, a simplified version of events will suffice to satisfy Miss Monkton."

None of this surprised me, for I knew of old that Holmes lost interest in a case from the moment it was solved. Also, he had little love for the country and much preferred the town, so that our return to Baker Street would now be uppermost in his mind.

A cloud of grey smoke hung heavily over the burnt-out stables. We saw the fire-cart departing down the drive, its work done. The sky was now fully light and clear. It would be a beautiful day.

We deposited Rawlings in the Great Hall with his legs strapped together and went in search of Miss Monkton, first encountering Walters who displayed considerable dismay until Holmes instructed him to set off for Armington Magna again immediately.

Miss Monkton was discovered still in her aunt's chamber. At our knock she threw open the door and expressed great relief at our safety, and at our news that the fears of her aunt and herself were finally at an end. With a flash of her fiery spirit, she insisted on confronting Rawlings.

And so the jester performed for the last time. At the sight of her, Rawlings realised he had been duped, and his obscene tongue was without restraint. He writhed upon the flagstones and foamed at the mouth, while snarling hatred through bared teeth.

Presently, Walters brought Sergeant Grimes to take charge of the prisoner. Shortly after, a wagon with barred windows drawn by black horses arrived, and Rawlings was taken to a local police cell to await the coming of Lestrade. Holmes insisted that we should ride with the party, so that the prisoner never left our sight until he was behind bars with the key withdrawn from the lock.

A shortened version of the jester's crimes and capture was dictated to Constable Peters, who wrote down every word laboriously while the sergeant looked on.

Lestrade arrived on the mid-day train. Holmes re-told the story, promising to fill in the details when they next met in London. More than once, my friend had remarked to me on the extent of the help received from Scotland Yard in the solving of this case. It was their files, he said, that had truly brought about the outcome, and so Lestrade could justifiably claim the credit.

We returned briefly to Theobald Grange for our things, and farewells were soon over. Holmes politely cut short the gratitude of Miss Monkton who was already almost restored to the handsome young woman we encountered at Brenner's. Then, after leaving our good wishes for Lady Heminworth's early recovery, Walters drove us into Armington Magna in time for the late afternoon train.

An hour later, with the smoke billowing from the engine and the last of the lush Warwickshire countryside disappearing behind us, I watched Holmes as he sat with his eyes closed in the opposite seat of our first-class carriage.

"My congratulations, Watson," he said suddenly, surprising me as I had thought him asleep. "You have contained your impatience regarding the true extent of this affair admirably, while I rested briefly. Now I suppose I had better satisfy your curiosity, as best I can. If you ever see fit to write this for publication, pray do not over-dramatize everything, as you have done in your other somewhat exaggerated accounts. On this occasion, I have done little more than take the obvious action that the situation demanded. Kindly keep a reasonable perspective, and you shall know all that I have discovered."

At this I took up my notebook, as Holmes folded his arms across his chest.

"It was obvious from the first," he began, "that every action against the Heminworths had but a single concealed purpose. The murders, the terrorising of her Ladyship and the appearances of the ridiculous but deadly jester were a means to an end. The object of it all was to gain possession of one of the largest diamonds yet discovered in South Africa's Kimberley fields. Donald Heminworth called it the Eye of Africa."

"I recall your mention of it before."

"Quite. It seems that Heminworth won the gem in a game of cards with a group of good-natured but drunken miners. On having it valued, he realised that he held in his hands the means to restore his family to its former position. However, the man we know as Rawlings had sat in on that game also. He was at that time, and still is, a fugitive from the authorities in South Africa and elsewhere, wanted for several murders and other serious crimes. His temporary guise as a miner was for concealment while he planned his next enterprise, which proved to be the befriending of Donald Heminworth for his own ends.

"Eventually, Heminworth was persuaded by Rawlings to form a partnership, working a claim not far from the site where the Eye of Africa was originally discovered. Little else of value was found in the area. After some time Rawlings became impatient, for his partner resisted all his attempts to discuss the diamond, or its hiding place. One night Heminworth returned to his lodgings to find Rawlings ransacking his rooms, whereupon the two men fought with knives. Rawlings escaped, leaving Heminworth for dead.

"Several weeks later Heminworth left the hospital. The local men who had discovered and taken him there, now assisted him to arrange a passage to England. There was no news of Rawlings."

Holmes paused in his narrative, and I took the opportunity to ask a question: "If this is the truth of the matter, what was the shameful act that turned Sir Joseph against his son?"

My friend waited until the loud wail of the train's whistle had died away.

"That was another of Rawlings' outrages," he said then. "Although secretly a wanted criminal himself, he did not hesitate to register a charge of diamond smuggling against his former partner. He was desperate to keep Heminworth in South Africa, where he could more easily take the diamond from him. Also, he realised that Heminworth must carry it on his person, since he would never have left without it."

"Yet leave he did, for he arrived at Theobald Grange."

"The charge was brought after Heminworth sailed. As a result of his enquiries, Lestrade received word of this, but was reluctant to proceed without sufficient evidence. Sir Joseph, on the other hand, always a man of impeccable respectability and honour, considered the accusation to be a smear on the family name. It seems that Donald Heminworth had spent a rather wild youth, and his production of the stone confirmed his guilt, rather than disproved it, in his father's eyes. Sir Joseph was torn between his love for his son and fear of the scandal of his arrest as a common thief, especially if this were to take place in the family home."

"So he sent the young man away with the diamond, to Australia," I ventured.

"Sent him away, yes, but I will explain that later. However, it did not take long for Rawlings to follow him as far as England, and there he lost the scent."

I put down my pencil. "But how can all this be, Holmes, when Miss Monkton told us that McIlroy, who worked as groom at Theobald Grange for fifteen years, served with Rawlings in India?"

"When I collated the information from Lady Heminworth and Miss Monkton, with that obtained during casual conversations in the village, and most of all with Lestrade's generous contributions, I was forced to the conclusion that the Rawlings known to McIlroy is not the man we accompanied to a police cell this morning."

"An imposter?"

Holmes nodded. "I suspected this, and that there was an accomplice, quite early in our investigation. Perhaps, Watson, it will give you an impression of this man's ruthlessness and disregard for human life, if I explain something of his history."

"You evidently know all about him."

"My index at Baker Street was woefully inadequate in this instance, but Scotland Yard did not fail me. After a study of their files, I assembled the pieces of my theory, and waited for further knowledge and events to disprove it. In fact, the opposite occurred."

"I formed the impression that you identified our enemy quite soon."

"When I heard that the jester had knowledge of Lady Heminworth's unstable condition, of the family's history and of the disposition of their home, it became obvious that someone near at hand, or who had been so, was the culprit. There were therefore but three possibilities. Walters was immediately exonerated because of his age, which left only Grover and Rawlings. Our interview with Grover convinced me of his innocence, my only reservation being that he rushed to conceal something as we arrived at his cottage. Because he had, in the eyes of the law, a criminal past, I returned in his absence. I have already explained, I think, that my discoveries had no connection with the case. And so I was left with Rawlings and the only real difficulty, which was to obtain absolute proof."

"There was the mystery of the jester's flight."

"Ah yes, that too. But first a summary of our prisoner's career."

I waited with my pencil poised, as Holmes lit his pipe.

"You will recall Miss Monkton's account of the fate of Enoch Martindale?" He asked as he puffed out the first wreaths of smoke.

"Sir Joseph's butler? He drowned, I think she said. My God, Holmes, was he another of Rawlings" victims?"

"I have not the slightest doubt of it. As we were told, he spent much of his off-duty time at the tavern, indulging himself with excessive quantities of port. There, I am reliably informed by sources in addition to Miss Monkton, he made the acquaintance of Benjamin Crown, a travelling labourer. The two men began to meet regularly, and over many glasses of beer and port, exchanged stories of their experiences in life, as men do. Thus Crown became familiar with the situation at Theobald Grange. He learned of her Ladyship's deep interest in things mystical, as well as her nervous disposition, and of the family legend. The moment Martindale told of the impending arrival of Rawlings, McIlroy's friend and replacement, his fate was sealed."

"Was this Crown also the murderer of Sir Joseph and Robert Heminworth?" I asked as we entered a tunnel.

"Without doubt," my friend said in the darkness, "and of others before them, in South Africa. He was notorious there. When the time was right, he became the Rawlings that we know."

"Notorious? But I have not heard the name before."

"Like many skilled criminals, Crown is virtually unknown to the general public, but Lestrade's delight was evident as he took charge of him. You, Watson, may remember the Tessenheim Bank robbery, or the Wildener murders, from the accounts in the newspapers."

At this I was taken aback. "Those outrages were his work?

"I have said as much. But his most callous crime was the Doormeer kidnapping in the Transvaal. Two small children were left to die of exposure, despite his demands being met. That is how he came to be in South Africa at the same time as Donald Heminworth."

"That was inhuman!"

"Fortunately, the children were recovered in time." He rose and crossed the carriage to knock out his pipe through the half-open window. "So now, old friend, you know the sort of enemy we have faced, over these last few days. You will recall my repeated admonishments to expect attack from any quarter." He resumed his seat and leaned back against the cushion. "Crown used the information supplied unwittingly by Martindale to take the place of Rawlings."

"Ah, we come to that. What of the genuine Rawlings?"

We emerged into the light of day once more. Holmes had not moved, but sat in retrospection with his pipe held in front of him.

"Patience, Watson, first let us finish with the unfortunate Martindale. According to the coroner's report, he drowned in a water-filled ditch while in a drunken stupor. This would have been when Crown had extracted all he needed to pass himself off at the house."

"Of course! It had to be done, or he would have been recognised."

"Quite so. Yet he evidently has some talent for disguise, or someone in the village would have thought the face of Lady Heminworth's new groom to be familiar.

"First he had to dispose of McIlroy, whom Martindale had said was to leave for Aberdeen, two weeks before his replacement took up his duties. Doubtlessly, Crown meant to deal with him here, but as it was McIlroy left early and managed to complete the journey. However, he spent only a few hours in Scotland, before he was knocked down and killed by a coach. At the time it was thought to be accidental, although the coach was never traced."

"But in fact, Crown had followed him?"

"Of course. The risk of McIlroy ever returning to Theobald Grange and discovering the false Rawlings was slight indeed, but sufficient for Crown to act. It is that sort of efficiency that has ensured his long success as an international criminal. He is involved with no gang, and makes few errors."

"It has been some time, Holmes, since you have been matched against such an opponent."

"And glad I am of it! The world could never have too few men of that sort."

"Indeed. But what became of the real Rawlings?" I asked again.

"As far as I am aware, his body has never been found." Holmes said with a frown. "He probably lies in an unmarked grave in a farmer's field or somewhere beneath the forest floor in the area surrounding Armington Magna. Do you recall Walters' story about the arrival of a letter from Kent which Rawlings, as we then knew him, destroyed in anger?"

"I do, and my failure to tell you of it."

He smiled. "That is of no consequence, for in retrospect I could have done nothing. The letter was to inform Rawlings of his mother's impending visit. She was to have stayed in Armington Magna."

"Exposure would have been immediate."

"Quite. You will remember the elderly woman found dead near the station. It is certain that Crown met her from the train."

"It seems there is no end to his crimes."

"He is without compassion, certainly. The reason for his assaults on Lady Heminworth's sanity was to induce Donald Heminworth to return, so that he would surrender the diamond to save his mother."

"But how would he hear of the affair, in Australia?"

"Donald Heminworth is not in Australia. I promised to tell you the truth about his banishment, and that is it. That is why her Ladyship would never speak of it to anyone, because of the possibility that the jester was somewhere in the house, within earshot."

"Yet he found out, or else he would have sailed for Australia rather than begin a reign of terror here."

"It was an unguarded moment, perhaps. A careless word spoken by Lady Heminworth or Sir Joseph."

"So, he had only to dispose of Sir Joseph and Robert Heminworth, for her Ladyship to be at his mercy. Truly, no man was ever more deserving of a rope around his neck."

"And he shall have it," said Holmes with a grim smile. "Although, it grieves me that his accomplices have escaped justice."

"You have not yet explained about Farraday."

"He was no better." My friend's expression hardened. "You are aware of course, that it was he you encountered in the wine cellar. Immediately afterwards, you met Crown in the guise of Rawlings, which convinced you of his innocence."

"I still thought we had but one opponent."

"Of course, and your conviction was reinforced by seeing the jester escape across the fields, moments before Crown appeared from a different direction."

"Exactly that."

"As we discovered later, Farraday was on his way to a rendezvous with Blackthorne and Cairns who were paid participants in these crimes. That is why they were silenced as soon as their usefulness was exhausted and their knowledge had become dangerous. Besides, it is doubtful that Crown intended to share the proceeds of his crime with anyone."

"Would he have murdered Farraday then, had they been successful?"

"That was to be expected, for Crown has always worked alone. I believe that Farraday's introduction to crime was when he murdered Ivan Barcherov, his fellow performer at the circus. Farraday had become discontent with life as an aerialist, for it was dangerous work for little reward. When Barcherov told him of the savings he had amassed for his return to Russia, the temptation proved too great. Sometime later, possibly at a tavern or eating-house, Farraday met Crown much as Martindale had. By now the plan to terrorize Lady Heminworth had formed in Crown's mind, but on hearing of Farraday's profession, he realized how dramatically its effects could be enhanced. He was no acrobat, so it is likely that his original intentions were different, but how the two

199

men acquainted each other with their past murders and revealed their mutual willingness to kill again will always be something of a mystery."

"Could it not be that Crown obtained Farraday's assistance by blackmailing him over Barcherov's murder?"

Holmes considered this. "Possibly. Farraday may have confided in his new friend, or revealed his secret while the worse for drink. The question is academic however, since both men are equally reprehensible in this affair."

"Last night, as I fought with him, Crown said that the diamond was his property, and that he was trying to retrieve it."

"Yet there is no question that Donald Heminworth won it fairly. News travels fast in those small mining communities, and a card cheat would have quickly been regarded as a leper. Remember that it was a group of miners who transported him to hospital and arranged for his passage back to England. No, Watson, Crown's only claim to the gem was based on the considerable criminal effort he had expended to gain possession of it."

A vibration passed quickly through the coach, causing us to fall silent while the train crossed a set of points. I waited until the mesmeric throb of the wheels resumed.

"There must be more to this man than even you have discovered," I said then. "I saw his mocking arrogance after his capture. How much more crime could be laid at his door? He has vowed to reveal nothing, so we may never know."

Holmes' eyes shone with a harsh glitter. "Many a hardened criminal has sought absolution by confession, at the sight of the hangman's rope."

I nodded. "Perhaps his tongue will loosen when he stands upon the gallows. When did you first realise who we were up against?"

"You will recall our first conversation with Crown, or Rawlings, near the stables?"

"Vividly."

"The coughing spasm that you were so concerned about was intended as a distraction, to cover up his surprise at our appearance. He was caught off guard, and reverted to his original speech for an instant, but it was enough for me to recognise the harsh lilt of the Boer. Remembering that Donald Heminworth had arrived home from South Africa, I saw at once the first link in our chain of deduction. When he spoke again, after his supposed recovery, it was with no trace of his previous accent. Still I made no further connection, having at the time only limited knowledge of Crown's exploits, but I was aware that he knew I had noticed his mistake. I was therefore prepared for an attempt on my life, and possibly on yours. His identity was confirmed to my satisfaction when he interrupted our meal during the storm, to tell us of Grover's visitor."

"A crude attempt to divert suspicion?" I suggested.

"And a way of separating us, by luring me out of the house. He knew that I would investigate alone, for you would certainly remain in the house to protect the women. I believe that I had posed an increasing threat to his plans for too long. A short distance from the house I noticed him waiting in the trees, probably with a garrotting wire or heavy club, but the concealment of the wood and the storm helped me to evade him as far as Grover's house. At that point or shortly after when I met Grover and his friend on the road, I think our murderer abandoned his intentions temporarily. It was the sight of this stranger, earlier, that gave Crown the notion of using him as a decoy, and of course the man would have made an ideal scapegoat for my murder."

"But how did Crown's intrusion at Theobald Grange identify him to you?"

"He was soaking wet."

"I cannot see what difference that makes."

Holmes surprise at my lack of comprehension was evident. "His ears, Watson, his ears. His hair was stuck down, revealing them."

"Ah! They stood out from his head."

"True, but more noticeably their tops were missing. No doubt he received punishment for some past crime from a source other than the law."

"So, while in London, you examined Scotland Yard's files for a man with such mutilations?"

He nodded his assent. "Despite some alterations to his appearance, I recognised his portrait at once. My worst fears as to the ruthless and pitiless nature of our adversary were confirmed in that instant."

We fell silent as the train came to a halt at a busy station. Passengers alighted and others boarded, their bustling movements a distraction until well after we were in open country again, gathering speed.

"Holmes?" I looked up from my notes. "Why did Donald Heminworth not return to Theobald Grange at the news of the deaths of his father and brother?"

He gave up his study of the passing countryside, turning from the window to face me. "Her Ladyship went to great lengths to keep any knowledge of the murders from him. All newspaper references to the tragedies was successfully suppressed by the use of her influence. She was aware that the publication of what had transpired would bring her son back by the first train. As you know, in London we were ignorant of the entire situation before the appearance of Miss Monkton. You will recall my mentioning that my index was of little use, since the newspapers held no information."

"Lady Heminworth is a resourceful woman, yet it was her fear of the supernatural that gave Crown his opportunity."

"Such a man would have found other means to conduct his reign of terror, had she not possessed such vulnerabilities. He also is resourceful, and I am convinced that it was his meeting with Farraday that prompted him to make use of the family legend. Had Lady Heminworth remained with us to the end, I could have pointed out that ghosts do not attack mortals with weapons of steel and wood, as the jester did you, nor can they be wounded by revolver bullets."

"Quite so," I smiled. "I imagine the discovery of the parchment did much to condition her for what was to come?"

"She believed it to be authentic. However, the British Museum denounced it quite quickly."

"You took it to London?" I retorted when I had grasped his meaning. "I was under the impression that it was left in the library."

"Walters watched as I finished with it and put it away, but I have some little knowledge of sleight-of-hand that enabled me to transfer it to my pocket without being observed. The museum curator was highly amused by the manuscript, since in his experience it was a poor forgery. I returned it to its place on my return, after ascertaining that it had not been missed."

"So the discovery in the East Tower was no more than a cunning device to introduce the concept of the long-dead and vengeful jester to her Ladyship?"

"My researches have revealed that the manner of death of Baron Roger de Lorme's jester, as represented to us, is a matter of historical record. It is also true that Theobald Grange stands on the exact site of the former Armington Keep. There, however, the story ends. I could find no record of a curse. To a man as conversant with the criminal underworld as Crown surely is, it must have been a simple matter to have the parchment artificially aged by chemical means. To find someone who could inscribe it with script barely recognisable to us, cleverly entwining historical fact with his own fiction, would also have presented him with little difficulty. The subsequent appearances of the jester would no doubt have increased to some sort of crescendo, possibly another murder, until Lady Heminworth could stand no more. She would then call upon her son to produce the diamond, and Crown would be watching for his arrival. All this was intended before we appeared on the scene, but I believe we altered the situation somewhat."

"Had we not done so, how many other lives might have been forfeited?" We braced ourselves against our seats as the train entered a sharp curve. "This has been a grim story, Holmes, from the outset."

"I would not care to be presented with another of its kind, just yet." His voice was heavy with weariness, and I knew that the strain of this affair was beginning to take its toll. "But now that this rather haphazard commentary is finished," he stifled a yawn, "and as an hour or so remains before we arrive at Paddington, we can attempt to reclaim some of our lost sleep. Afterwards, since this singular adventure began at Brenner's, I see no reason why it should not end there also."

Also from MX Publishing

MX Publishing is the world's largest specialist Sherlock Holmes publisher, with over a hundred titles and fifty authors creating the latest in Sherlock Holmes fiction and non-fiction.

From traditional short stories and novels to travel guides and quiz books, MX Publishing cater for all Holmes fans.

The collection includes leading titles such as _Benedict Cumberbatch In Transition_ and _The Norwood Author_ which won the 2011 Howlett Award (Sherlock Holmes Book of the Year).

MX Publishing also has one of the largest communities of Holmes fans on Facebook with regular contributions from dozens of authors.

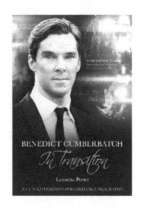

www.mxpublishing.com

Also from MX Publishing

 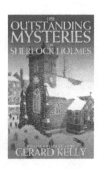 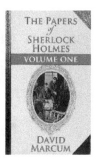

Our bestselling books are our short story collections;

"Lost Stories of Sherlock Holmes" , "The Outstanding
Mysteries of Sherlock Holmes", The Papers of Sherlock
Holmes Volume 1 and 2, "Untold Adventures of Sherlock
Holmes" (and the sequel "Studies in Legacy) and "Sherlock
Holmes in Pursuit", "The Cotswold Werewolf and Other
Stories of Sherlock Holmes" – and many more……

www.mxpublishing.com

Also from MX Publishing

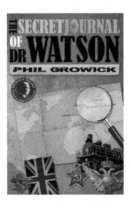

"Phil Growick's, "The Secret Journal of Dr. Watson", is an adventure which takes place in the latter part of Holmes and Watson's lives. They are entrusted by HM Government (although not officially) and the King no less to undertake a rescue mission to save the Romanovs, Russia's Royal family from a grisly end at the hand of the Bolsheviks. There is a wealth of detail in the story but not so much as would detract us from the enjoyment of the story. Espionage, counter-espionage, the ace of spies himself, double-agents, double-crossers...all these flit across the pages in a realistic and exciting way. All the characters are extremely well-drawn and Mr. Growick, most importantly, does not falter with a very good ear for Holmesian dialogue indeed. Highly recommended. A five-star effort."
The Baker Street Society

www.mxpublishing.com

Also from MX Publishing

The Missing Authors Series

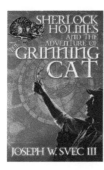  

Sherlock Holmes and The Adventure of The Grinning Cat
Sherlock Holmes and The Nautilus Adventure
Sherlock Holmes and The Round Table Adventure

"Joseph Svec, III is brilliant in entwining two endearing and enduring classics of literature, blending the factual with the fantastical; the playful with the pensive; and the mischievous with the mysterious. We shall, all of us young and old, benefit with a cup of tea, a tranquil afternoon, and a copy of Sherlock Holmes, The Adventure of the Grinning Cat."
Amador County Holmes Hounds Sherlockian Society

www.mxpublishing.com

Also from MX Publishing

The American Literati Series

 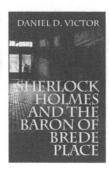 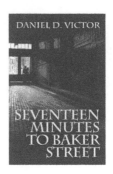

The Final Page of Baker Street
The Baron of Brede Place
Seventeen Minutes To Baker Street

"The really amazing thing about this book is the author's ability to call up the "essence" of both the Baker Street "digs" of Holmes and Watson as well as that of the "mean streets" of Marlowe's Los Angeles. Although none of the action takes place in either place, Holmes and Watson share a sense of camaraderie and self-confidence in facing threats and problems that also pervades many of the later tales in the Canon. Following their conversations and banter is a return to Edwardian England and its certainties and hope for the future. This is definitely the world before The Great War."
Philip K Jones

www.mxpublishing.com

Also from MX Publishing

The Detective and The Woman Series

The Detective and The Woman
The Detective, The Woman and The Winking Tree
The Detective, The Woman and The Silent Hive

"The book is entertaining, puzzling and a lot of fun. I believe the author has hit on the only type of long-term relationship possible for Sherlock Holmes and Irene Adler. The details of the narrative only add force to the romantic defects we expect in both of them and their growth and development are truly marvelous to watch. This is not a love story. Instead, it is a coming-of-age tale starring two of our favorite characters."
Philip K Jones

www.mxpublishing.com

Also from MX Publishing

The Sherlock Holmes and Enoch Hale Series

 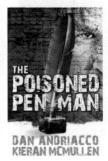 

The Amateur Executioner
The Poisoned Penman
The Egyptian Curse

"The Amateur Executioner: Enoch Hale Meets Sherlock Holmes", the first collaboration between Dan Andriacco and Kieran McMullen, concerns the possibility of a Fenian attack in London. Hale, a native Bostonian, is a reporter for London's Central News Syndicate - where, in 1920, Horace Harker is still a familiar figure, though far from revered. "The Amateur Executioner" takes us into an ambiguous and murky world where right and wrong aren't always distinguishable. I look forward to reading more about Enoch Hale."
Sherlock Holmes Society of London

www.mxpublishing.com

Also from MX Publishing

Sherlock Holmes novellas in verse

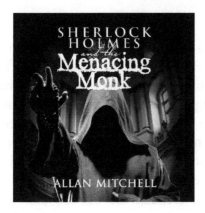

All four novellas
have been
released also in
audio format
with narration
by Steve White

Sherlock Holmes and The Menacing Moors
Sherlock Holmes and The Menacing Metropolis
Sherlock Holmes and The Menacing Melbournian
Sherlock Holmes and The Menacing Monk

"The story is really good and the Herculean effort it must have been to write it all in verse—well, my hat is off to you, Mr. Allan Mitchell! I wouldn't dream of seeing such work get less than five plus stars from me..." **The Raven**

Also from MX Publishing

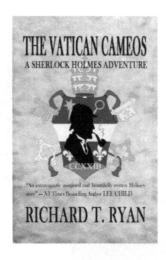

When the papal apartments are burgled in 1901, Sherlock Holmes is summoned to Rome by Pope Leo XII. After learning from the pontiff that several priceless cameos that could prove compromising to the church, and perhaps determine the future of the newly unified Italy, have been stolen, Holmes is asked to recover them. In a parallel story, Michelangelo, the toast of Rome in 1501 after the unveiling of his Pieta, is commissioned by Pope Alexander VI, the last of the Borgia pontiffs, with creating the cameos that will bedevil Holmes and the papacy four centuries later. For fans of Conan Doyle's immortal detective, the game is always afoot. However, the great detective has never encountered an adversary quite like the one with whom he crosses swords in "The Vatican Cameos."

"An extravagantly imagined and beautifully written Holmes story"
(Lee Child, NY Times Bestselling author, Jack Reacher series)

.

Lightning Source UK Ltd.
Milton Keynes UK
UKHW02f2157260318
320047UK00005B/170/P

9 781787 051867